The Ultimatum

Jennifer Wade

First published by Dog Ear Publishing
4010 W. 86th Street, Ste H
Indianapolis, IN 46268
www.dogearpublishing.net

ISBN: 978-145750-324-5

Printed in the United States of America

This book is dedicated in loving memory of Donna, our real-life Rachel. Although this story does not depict her life, it does chronicle the struggle she faced every day with lupus. We love you and we miss you more every day, but we know that we will see you in "a couple of hours."

Donna Burton
October 8, 1966–February 13, 2009
For more information on lupus, please visit the Lupus Foundation of America's web site:
www.lupus.org

He slipped quickly and quietly through the streets of Heaven. Around him shone the Light of the Son. He was in the Holy City, and in the distance, he could see a huge single pearl, one of the twelve gates of Heaven. The gates were part of the massive wall surrounding the city that glittered brilliantly with the gems that the wall was constructed with. Brightly colored quartz combined with sapphire, agate, emerald, beryl, onyx, topaz, jacinth, and amethyst caught the light and threw brilliant hues all over the city.

The walkway he traveled on glimmered of gold so pure that it looked like yellow glass. All around him he could hear the praises to Christ. "Holy, holy, holy is the Lord God Almighty, Who was, Who is, and Who is coming," came the constant refrain. It was a sound he never tired of hearing, and although his glorious surroundings never ceased to amaze him, he was on a mission and had no time to dwell on them. He was heading to the Throne Room, for he had a meeting with God Himself. There was work to be done, and this conference was important to plan tonight's encounter. He couldn't fail. He couldn't even consider the possibility.

He turned and walked into the massive room, feeling God's presence like a wonderful heaviness all around him, surrounding him like a cloak. He allowed it to envelop him briefly before continuing. The room itself was intimidating. In the center, behind a sea so clear it resembled the finest crystal, was God's throne. Surrounding it were twenty-four smaller thrones, upon which sat twenty-four leaders wearing crowns of gold on their heads. He passed the seraphim, angels with six wings, who guarded the room, with respectful trepidation and stepped up to the Throne. He reverently knelt and lowered his face to the golden floor.

"Father," he said, raising his head enough to ask, "are we ready?"

"We are," was the answer, the voice bellowing through the room like a trumpet. "The grandmother is obedient. She is on her way to him as we speak. Her prayers are strong, and they will carry us through to the end of this journey." God waved his arm out to him indicating for him to stand.

"What of the man? What will be his reaction?" The angel was tense about his upcoming assignment, for his responsibility was great.

God paused, momentarily in thought. "Cynical. But he will see."

The angel had one more question. "What will be the cost they must pay for our endeavor?" This thought concerned the angel because he deeply cared for these people.

Tears filled God's eyes as He answered, "The price will be great. They will feel the sting of defeat and the grief of death, but the expense has been calculated and the deposit has been made. The rest is up to them. The grandmother must be vigilant and prepared, and he must accept my offer."

They spent the next several hours planning the night's objective. Angelic servants made sure that they were uninterrupted for this conference. Every detail must be perfect, every angle explored, every question answered. They had to be ready. This was a matter of life and death.

Finally, they finished, but God had one more assignment for His emissary. "Go now. I have a message for Lydia. Take it to her and then wait for the signal to come from Brandon. It won't be long now, and tomorrow we will celebrate the outcome."

"Yes, Father. May all go according to our plan." The angel bowed low again in deference and devotion to his sovereign and then made a quick departure. He had the weight of his assignment on his shoulders. He knew the importance, and he knew the risk, but he would not return without victory.

CHAPTER 1

Brandon Moore walked through his apartment door. He turned on the light and flipped through his mail, tossing it onto the side table without even comprehending what had been in his mailbox. His mind was working overtime, and it was on everything but the present. His grandmother was coming for a visit, and he dreaded the encounter.

Oh, he loved her. With all his heart, he adored her. Lydia Stevens had practically raised him after his own had mother died. Goodness knows, his no-good, alcoholic father only cared about his next bottle of Jack Daniel's. To him, Brandon was only "the boy" who was in the way and a pawn to hurt the other people in Brandon's life. Lydia had rescued Brandon from the mire of abuse his dad had forced him through, and she had tried her hardest to make a happy life for him.

With a sigh, Brandon flopped into the worn recliner. His day as a journalist had worn him out. His job took him to the worst parts of the city, and he had seen way too much. There was pain everywhere he looked. He had experienced too much. His own life had been one beating after another, both physically and emotionally. It had started in his younger years and continued into his teens. Life had finally settled down for him when he moved in with Lydia, but by that time, Brandon had been nothing more than a battle scar.

He hadn't seen Lydia for several years. After graduating from college, he had been offered the job at the *Journal*, a small paper that put out an issue twice a week, and had moved from his small town in Virginia to Miami, Florida. He had hoped that the change would firmly put the past behind him. The hot, sunny days had held an enormous appeal, but he had quickly tired of the beach and party scene, which seemed meaningless. But Lydia was coming now, and with her came the buried memories of his past.

Lydia was a devout Christian. Every day, she spent hours praying to God. A god that Brandon said wasn't there. How could He be? If He really did exist, then why had Brandon's life been so full of pain? If there really was a God Who loved him, then He surely had a funny way of showing it. Brandon felt bad for thinking this way. It seemed like he was betraying his mother. She had believed, like Lydia, and had praised God until the final breath had escaped her lungs and her heart had ceased to beat. The moment he lost his mom, Brandon felt completely alone and abandoned—abandoned not only by his mother but also by the God she served. What God would leave a child without the person he needed most in the world?

Brandon leaned forward and put his head in his hands. He couldn't allow himself to think about his mom. The wound, although years old, was still too deep and raw. Instead, he forced his thoughts onto more practical things. Lydia would be there in a few hours, and he had to get ready.

He pushed himself out of the chair and walked through his apartment. It was small, with a kitchen, living room, bathroom, and two bedrooms. The kitchen was barely big enough for a dinette table and four wire chairs. His sparse collection of pots and pans was stored under the sink, and a few mismatched plates and cups lined his cabinets. The refrigerator at least had fresh milk, and that alone was a miracle. Brandon had gone grocery shopping in preparation for Lydia's visit. He was unaccustomed to seeing the fridge so well stocked. The freezer contained a stack of frozen TV dinners, which was Brandon's usual fare.

At least the apartment was clean, not the normal bachelor's pad. He was rarely home, so the place stayed fairly tidy. His father had taught him to keep a house neat. Those lessons had been painful to learn, but cleaning was now a habit for him.

Brandon walked down the narrow hall into the second bedroom, the one that Lydia would use. The tiny room was packed with a bed, a dresser, and an overstuffed chair. With all of those in the room, there was barely enough space left to move. But the sheets were new, bought for the occasion, and the carpet freshly vacuumed. Brandon had even brought in an arrangement of lilies, Lydia's favorite flowers, and placed them on the dresser. He changed direction and headed back to the kitchen.

Brandon knew that Lydia loved pot roast. He didn't cook much, but he did know how to fix that simple meal. He had sat at his grandmother's table and watched her prepare it for him on many occasions. He started on the menial task of peeling and cutting potatoes, carrots, and onions. Once that was done, he added the roast, water, and seasonings, covered it, and put it in the oven to bake. He removed some rolls from the freezer and placed them on the counter to thaw. He would fix them later so they would still be hot when he and his grandmother ate. Upon completing that task, he realized that he was still restless. He decided to shower and then fill the rest of the time watching television. Perhaps he could get lost in some mindless sitcom while he waited.

Two hours later, Brandon was surprised that time had passed faster than he had expected it to. The food was ready, and the TV programs had actually gotten his mind off of things. The doorbell rang, and with mixed feelings of anticipation and apprehension, he rose to answer it.

Lydia Stevens leaned her head against the seat of the airplane. She was filled with conflicting emotions concerning this trip, ranging from elation to trepidation to guilt. At seventy-one years old, she was a still a very active woman. Her favorite pastime was bowling, and she competed in a senior league at her local bowling alley. The regular activity kept her trim and fit. The practice also kept her playing well. She was considered her team's best bowler, a fact that she humbly accepted. But now she was on her way to see her grandson. Lydia sighed as she absently pushed a few straggling hairs back into their clip. Her shoulder-length hair had long ago turned from blonde to a pure white, and she kept it manageable by pulling it back.

Her thoughts returned to her grandson. This was a trip that made her apprehensive. She loved Brandon, and she desperately wanted to see him, but she also knew the importance of this visit. The Lord had told her to come. He had said that it was imperative for her to be there for Brandon because God had something for him. Lydia was to go to Florida and begin this mission, so she had bought her plane tickets and then informed Brandon of her visit.

She had known that Brandon would try to talk her out of coming, and he had tried. He tried to tell her that the timing was bad and he was very busy at work. Lydia knew that it was probably true, but Brandon had given in, as she had known he would, when he had learned that she had already invested her money in airline reservations.

In many ways, Brandon was still a child trying to earn love and feeling responsible for everyone around him. Lydia realized that there was tension between the two of them, and she knew where it came from. She sighed and absently pushed her glasses farther up on the bridge of her nose. Brandon had led a rough life and been forced to grow up way too quickly. His mother, Lydia's only child, had taught him about Jesus. Brandon had even once believed. But his mother had been very ill; she had suffered with systematic lupus that affected her immune system. She had developed lung cancer, a complication of the disease, and had passed away when Brandon was only twelve years old. Her death, and the events that had taken place after it, had driven a wedge between Brandon and God that had become a deep chasm over the years.

Lydia carried Brandon to Christ in her prayers every day. On her knees, she wept and pleaded for God to intervene, so when He had said, "Go!" Lydia had obeyed without question. Nevertheless, Brandon and Lydia had grown apart over the years, and it was all due to their stark difference in faith. Lydia understood that this would be a reunion of mixed emotions.

The seatbelt light flashed, and Lydia felt the plane start its slow descent. In just a few minutes, she would be leaving the security of the airplane and stepping out into the unknown. The weight of her burden was almost too great to bear. The plane finished its descent and soon stopped on the runway. Lydia sighed as she rose from her seat and collected her belongings from the overhead compartment. She hadn't checked her bags. Several years ago, her luggage had been lost, an incident she didn't want repeated. Because this wouldn't be a very long visit, she had decided not to risk another mishap. Furthermore, not having to wait for her things would save her time inside the busy airport.

"Help me, Lord. I've come this far. Carry me for the rest of my journey," she prayed as she filed into the terminal with the others from her flight.

She saw her name on white poster board, held up by the taxi driver she had requested. She had called the company before she left home, given them the flight number and arrival time, and asked to be met by someone. Lydia knew that Brandon would have gladly picked her up; however, she had felt the need to have just a few more moments to herself before she faced Brandon and their past.

Lydia walked toward the young man who was to be her driver. He smiled as she approached and opened the door for her. He was in his mid to late twenties, about Brandon's age. His blonde hair reminded her of spun gold and had just a hint of a wave. He was much taller than average and had a stocky build. She assumed that many young girls would fall for the impish grin he gave her as he shut the car door after she had lowered herself into the front seat. As she settled into the worn interior, the young man loaded her bag in the trunk, then sat beside her. He turned the key in the ignition as she gave him Brandon's address.

"How was your flight today, ma'am?" he asked politely. She was struck by the deep tone of his voice. It was very comforting, and she liked him immediately.

"It was nice. Tiring, but nice," she responded politely. The cab was old, but it was apparently kept very well. The interior was clean, there was no smell of cigarette smoke, and the leather on the dash shone like it had just been polished.

"Are you in town visiting?" he continued.

"Yes." Lydia looked at the driver's ID card that hung on the mirror of the car. "Simeon. That's an unusual name."

"Yes ma'am," he agreed, "but it suits me well." He threw her a smile, and she could again see how attractive he probably was to the young ladies. She mulled his name over again in her mind.

"I like it."

The conversation stalled, and the next several minutes were kept in affable silence. They pulled into the parking lot of Brandon's building and stopped in front of the main door.

"I'll unload your things, ma'am, then I'll carry them to the apartment."

"No need, Simeon. It's only one lightweight bag, and I'm not going far. The apartment is on the second floor."

"If that's what you wish," Simeon replied. He opened the car door for her, helped her out, and then went to the back of the car. Lydia waited by the apartment building's entrance. She took a moment to survey her surroundings. Brandon's apartment building was in a lower-income neighborhood but was well maintained. There were flowers planted in mulch lining the sidewalks, and the grass around the building was neat and tidy. She could hear the gentle singing of birds nesting in the nearby trees. She noticed security cameras mounted on the wall, but the area looked as though crime didn't touch it often. There was no graffiti painted on any of the surrounding buildings, and there were no bars on the windows. The neighborhood seemed to be generally safe. Lydia jumped as Simeon came up behind her, placing the strap of her luggage in her hand. Before she could turn to thank him, he leaned in to her ear and whispered, "Tonight is a night for miracles, Lydia. Pray for Brandon. The war has started, and it will be settled before morning. He will need to feel your quiet strength and to know that you are fighting for him. God is with you."

Lydia was startled. She knew the taxi driver had her name from her reservation, but she had never mentioned Brandon's name or the reason for her visit. She whirled to ask the man how he knew her grandson. With a cry, she realized that he was gone, and so was the taxi. What had just happened? In a daze, she took her luggage and walked to Brandon's apartment door. She raised her hand and knocked.

CHAPTER 2

Brandon stood in the doorway and looked at his grandmother. Although she was older than when he had last seen her and there were new lines surrounding Lydia's eyes and mouth, the years had been very kind. Brandon was surprised that tears filled his eyes and the emotion nearly choked him. Even though their relationship was strained, it was good to see her. He took a step toward her, and she fell into his embrace. He knew that this reunion was as hard on her as it was on him. He understood why her tears were soaking his shirt. He was struggling to keep his own tears from dropping down his face. It had been too long since they had been together, and it felt wonderful to hold her.

The two finally separated and walked into the apartment. He took her bag and carried them to the spare bedroom. He took a moment to compose himself before going back into the living room. He smiled as he saw Lydia making herself at home in his sparse kitchen. She had already found the dishes and utensils and was serving dinner for the two of them. She looked up as Brandon entered the room. "I thought that you might make a roast for dinner tonight. I'm glad. It's always been a favorite of mine," she commented.

"I know. You taught me how to fix it. I only hope that it is as good as yours. But I seriously doubt it. You have always ruled the kitchen."

They took their plates and sat down at the table. Brandon lifted the fork to his mouth but then caught Lydia's eye. He could see the tension appearing on her face, and he hated knowing that he was the cause of it.

"Do you mind if I pray?" she asked quietly. She had steeled herself for an argument, but Brandon refused to disagree with her this early in her visit. He decided to let her have her way this time.

"Go ahead. I'll wait until you're finished."

He saw her gratefulness and was pleased. So what if he didn't believe? Why should it matter to him if she did? Maybe they could become close again if he just avoided the arguments of his youth. He hated the division that resulted from the constant conflict, so he decided to compromise. He made a resolution to himself to just keep his opinions on faith to himself. That would certainly make this time with his grandmother more enjoyable, and he really wanted a pleasant visit with her.

Lydia finished her prayer of thanks, and they ate while filling the quiet apartment with amiable small talk. Once they were finished, Brandon told Lydia to rest in the living room while he cleaned up. He knew she was tired from her flight—he could see it in her eyes—and there wasn't a huge mess anyway. He put the dirty dishes in the dishwasher, turned it on, and covered the leftovers. The meat would make excellent sandwiches for lunch tomorrow. After storing the food in the refrigerator, Brandon looked around the kitchen one last time. Satisfied that everything was in order, he made a pot of coffee and then, carrying two cups, went to join Lydia.

He found her comfortably sitting on the couch, with her feet propped up, holding his scrapbook of articles he had written. He knew that she had kept up with his career. She had subscribed to the *Journal* the day he had been hired. His editor, Mr. Evans, personally sent her the biweekly newspaper, saying that Lydia had impressed him when she had called in her subscription and that he wanted to make sure she could read Brandon's work. Lydia and Mr. Evans talked frequently over the phone and had become good, albeit long-distance, friends. Brandon knew that Mr. Evans was also a believer. He felt that Lydia had probably shared her concerns for Brandon with Mr. Evans in hopes that he could reach Brandon in her absence. But Mr. Evans never pushed. He would look at Brandon with compassion and Brandon knew he was praying for him, but Brandon felt that those prayers were useless. He knew better than anyone that no one was there to hear them.

Lydia looked up as Brandon sat in the chair across from the couch. She smiled. "I like your portfolio. You've done good work for the *Journal*," she commented. There was no mistaking the pride in her voice. "You really capture the emotions of the people you write about."

"That's what Mr. Evans wanted when he hired me," Brandon said. "He told me that there were enough hard-hitting journalists out there. He said he needed a person that could get to the bottom of a story and explain the impact felt by the people living the experiences."

"You've certainly done your job well. I'm extremely proud of you."

Brandon scowled at the comment. He loved his job, but sometimes the dark sentiments that he wrote about stayed in his mind for days and weeks. Brandon could feel the terror of a child injured in a drive-by shooting. He could empathize with the father losing his job and having his house foreclosed on, and he struggled with a way to make things right. All he could do was write a story and hope that by bringing awareness to a situation, he could open doors for help to come, somehow.

"Yeah, well. I guess living through some of the same things the people I write about gives me an advantage." Brandon couldn't stop the bitterness from creeping into his tone.

Lydia ignored the sarcasm. It was deserved. Brandon had lived through many of these situations himself. It was what helped him relate to people and better articulate their stories. Brandon would probably never realize how much his words helped victims through their grief. "You're right. You do know how it feels to get kicked while you're down better than most people." Lydia's response was quiet, sympathetic.

Brandon quickly changed the subject. "What have you been doing? I assume you're still bowling better than everyone else at the alley?"

"That's what they tell me," she said with a laugh. "By the way, do you remember Dory?"

Brandon grinned. "The little blue-haired lady that tried to bowl with you but kept putting the ball in the gutters?" In his mind, he could see the short, slightly heavy woman with silver hair tinged with blue bobbing toward the lane and grappling her bowling ball. He laughed out loud as he remembered her habit of biting her tongue in concentration.

Lydia giggled as she remembered those days. Dory had been hard to teach, but she was a wonderful lady and pure joy to have around. "Yes. That's her. We finally taught her how to follow through on her release. She's doing much better now. But she told me to tell you hello and to come back soon. She said she misses your hugs and she wants one."

They both fell quiet as they thought of earlier times. Brandon used to love going to the bowling alley with Lydia. He would watch as she bowled with her teammates. Lydia was always the life of the party, and the women on her team spent the entire time laughing and joking. After her team was finished, Lydia would stay behind and bowl with Brandon. When he was fifteen, she had bought him his own bowling ball and he had joined a youth league. With Lydia's instruction, he had gotten to be very good, but he had never beaten her. He suddenly had a thought.

"Gram, there is a new bowling alley in town, and I've heard good things about it. Would you like to go one evening while you are here? I haven't bowled since I moved down here from Virginia," he said.

Lydia smiled. "I would love to. I couldn't bring my ball, but I'm sure there are some there that I can use. What about you? Do you still have your bowling ball?"

"Of course. I kept hoping that I would get a chance to use it sometime, but there hasn't been much time for fun," he remarked. He thought about the ball in his closet. It was his favorite gift from Lydia because of all the good memories attached to it. He did have a few good memories hovering in his past, and bowling with his gram made some of the best.

They lapsed into silence again. Haltingly, Brandon approached the subject that he knew would cause tension. "Gram," he asked cautiously, "why did you come? The true reason?"

Lydia placed her coffee cup on the side table and thought for several moments before answering. "Brandon, I will tell you," she began, "but you won't like hearing it. Are you sure you want my answer?"

Brandon braced himself. "Go ahead. We need to get past this, and the sooner we do, the better the rest of your time here will be."

Lydia paused again before answering honestly. "Quite frankly, I came because God told me to. He said that He had something for you and I needed to be here to support you. This was confirmed to me the moment I got here, but I will have to tell you about that later. You're not ready yet, and you wouldn't believe me."

Brandon was agitated. He had expected that this surprise visit had something to do with God, but he hadn't expected to hear Lydia say it out loud. He should have been prepared, but he wasn't. What shocked him the most was the strange feeling that he had when she proclaimed that God had sent her here for a specific reason, and that was him. It was like a kick in the gut, this mixture of anger and happiness, rejection and yet longing. Brandon couldn't explain it, so he got up and paced the room.

Lydia interrupted his thoughts. "Brandon, I know that you don't like this, but please hear what I say."

Brandon remembered his promise to himself over dinner. He would politely listen, and then he would ignore Lydia's advice.

"God loves you very much. He knows that you have had a rough life. When God created man, he gave us a free will. Your father had a choice, just like you do. He chose wrong, and you suffered the consequences at his hand. But God cannot take away our freedom to choose our own paths. What He can do, and what He does, is to surround us with His love as we endure the actions of someone else's wrong decisions."

Tears of anger mixed with frustration rose and spilled out of Brandon's eyes. Once again, he was shocked by the longing in his heart for Lydia's words to be true. He knew that they weren't true, though, and the disappointment was crushing. "What about my mother? Was it her free will to die and leave me alone? I was only twelve years old. My father was, and still is, a good-for-nothing drunk. He spent years terrorizing us. Mom finally left, and he left me alone until she died. Then he suddenly resurfaced, bringing nothing but pain. I had hoped for a father, but what I got was a monster." Brandon paused, his anger barely controlled. He could see the tears in Lydia's eyes. They made him feel guilty, but he ignored the feeling and continued talking.

"Okay, I see your point about his free will. But how could God allow my mother to be taken away? Was that her will? The courts decided that I was safe with my dad. I was there for two years before a boiling point was reached and you finally were able to convince a judge that I should be with you. Do you know what those years were like? How could you? You weren't around either. Dad had banned you from having contact with me." He hesitated briefly before continuing. "God couldn't allow these things, because He doesn't exist. It's a fantasy world, Gram. If it makes you happy, fine, believe that God is there and He cares about you. I just happen to know it's not true."

Now that he had finished his tirade, tears were streaming down both of their faces. Brandon felt like a disobedient little boy again. He berated himself for breaking his promise and falling apart. He knew that his remarks had cut Gram's heart deep, but he couldn't help how he felt. He watched Lydia as she took a deep breath, wiped her tears from her face, and stood.

She pulled her shoulders back, raising herself to her full height, and crossed the room until she stood directly in front of him. He towered over her by almost a foot, but right now, she seemed as tall as he was. She lifted her hands, gently cupping his face, and stared into his eyes.

"Brandon, I do know the hardships you have had in your life. You lost your mother, and I lost my daughter. Rachel was my life, and she left me too. But she loved God, and I know that I will see her again. God has her in His care until then. Whether you believe me or not, God is there, and He does love you. He told me to pray for you, and that is what I am going to do. Goodnight, Brandon. I will see you in the morning." Lydia turned and walked determinedly out of the room.

Brandon knew it was crazy—after all, Lydia had just gone to bed. She hadn't left his apartment or stepped out of his life, but he felt abandoned all over again just the same. Not knowing what else to do, he took the coffee cups with their cold contents to the kitchen sink and then went to bed as well.

CHAPTER 3

Lydia stood in her bedroom, trying to regain her composure. Leaving Brandon in the midst of an argument had been terribly hard. She knew, however, that she had done the right thing. Years ago, she had let the difference in faith tear them apart, but not this time.

She took a few moments and surveyed the bedroom. She smiled as her eyes hit the lilies on the dresser. She walked over and pulled one from the bouquet. She pressed it to her face and inhaled the flower's rich aroma. After this visit was over, she would take this lily home and press it in her Bible. She knew that something good was going to happen. God had promised her, and He never broke a promise. She just didn't know the price she and Brandon would have to pay to see the promise fulfilled.

A slight laugh escaped her lips when she looked at her bed. It was perfectly made with pink sheets. She knew that they were brand new, bought just for her.

Brandon had remembered her favorite color, just as he had remembered her favorite flower. The love in the gifts touched her heart. It was proof that, grown man that he was, he was still her little boy. Lydia knew he was grown up with adult responsibilities and opinions, but he still carried the pain of his childhood in his heart. It was a wound that would not heal quickly or easily.

Lydia knew how much Rachel's death had affected Brandon. It had nearly destroyed her too. She had found her strength in God, whereas Brandon had pushed Him away and buried his grief. She was confident that he would have turned around if his dad hadn't jerked him away. She had never asked Brandon what had happened during their two years of separation, because she hadn't wanted to know. But she had seen the changes in him when she had finally won custody. Robert had never wanted Brandon; he had just wanted to hurt Lydia. Robert had cursed everything that Rachel had held dear and had sabotaged every relationship Robert had with his alcohol abuse. The first time Lydia had lain eyes on Brandon after their separation, she barely recognized him. He was sullen and angry. He had withdrawn tightly into himself and refused to let anyone near. His eyes had been wary, and the defensive expression rarely left his face. Lydia's heart had nearly shattered, and she had set out to give him the happy life he deserved. Brandon had improved over time, but the sadness never completely left his eyes. She could still see it, lingering, even now.

Lydia's thoughts snapped back to the present. Her determination steeled her as she knelt on the floor. She lowered her face to the carpet and began crying out to God as her tears coursed down her cheeks and landed on the floor beneath her. It was time to do battle. There was a war going on and Brandon was the prize. With her prayers, Lydia readied herself and stepped into the fray.

Brandon closed the door to his bedroom. He wished he drank, but he hadn't had a taste for strong drink since he was in college. One bad incident had completely taken care of that urge. Brandon refused to be like his father, dependent on the stuff. Brandon didn't want the liquor right now; he just wanted the glass to throw against the wall. He settled for flinging the pillow off his bed and onto the floor. It didn't make him feel better. He walked across the room to recover the thrown pillow. It had landed directly in front of the handmade rocking chair in the corner facing Brandon's closet. Unconsciously, Brandon closed the closet door. The latch didn't work properly, and it kept popping open.

He didn't think it was possible to feel worse. Even with all the abuse and pain he had lived through, it paled in comparison to the guilt of hurting Lydia. He knew she was in her room, crying. He could hear it.

He could also hear her praying. She wasn't loud; he couldn't actually make out what she was saying, but the walls were thin and the sound carried through them.

He flopped on his bed, clasping his hands behind his head, and recounted the argument. He really had meant to just listen and let her have her opinion without getting upset, but the evening, just like his entire life, had failed to go according to his plan.

He remembered the day the judge had given custody of him to Lydia. He had been fourteen years old. His mom had been dead for two years, and he hadn't seen Lydia the entire time. His dad had kept telling Brandon that Lydia didn't care about him. At first, Brandon had argued with his father, but that had only resulted in a bloody nose or mouth, sometimes both. Eventually, Brandon had stopped arguing. He had pretty much steered clear of his dad, especially after Robert had been drinking, so Brandon went to school and came home. He would quickly clean the house and then hide in his room until he had no choice but to come out for supper, when there was food. Robert's booze always took priority over groceries. An education was Brandon's priority, even at a young age, so he continued to do his homework. He had always been a straight-A student, and he had refused to let the situation with his dad ruin that. If his teachers suspected a problem, they never asked. Then the day had come that brought the tension at home to a head.

Brandon was being honored for his grades at the eighth-grade graduation. Deep in his heart, he had hoped his dad would finally realize that he loved Brandon and would come. He desperately wanted his dad to be proud of him, but Robert had never come. It had been a foolish wish, anyway. Emotionally wounded, Brandon had walked the six blocks to his rundown house, practicing what he would say to his dad when he saw him.

"Dad," he would say, "I know we've had our troubles. But I love you. I know that Mom loved you too. I hoped that you could have seen me get that award. I'm trying hard to make you proud."

He had walked through the door, found his dad sleeping off a hangover, and gotten out one word before feeling the sting of his dad's belt across his back. In his haste to get to school that morning and his excitement about the ceremony, he had forgotten to make his bed. What resulted was the worst beating Brandon had ever had in his life. When it was over, Brandon had known that he could no longer live like this. He had waited until his dad was passed out, drunk, and limped to the neighbor's house. His neighbor, an elderly woman who reminded Brandon of Lydia, had called the police. The police had come and arrested his dad, bringing an ambulance with them. Brandon had been in the hospital for three days with broken ribs and a concussion. Someone had contacted Lydia, who immediately filed for custody. Brandon hadn't known that she had been through the legal channels, trying to get Robert's parental rights terminated for the entire two years. The judge had scheduled a hearing for the day Brandon was released from the hospital. In the meantime, no one had been allowed to visit him, so the judge could hear from Brandon without pressure from anyone. Brandon had spoken to the judge privately and then waited until Lydia was granted custody and picked him up.

When she had opened the door to the waiting room and he had seen her for the first time since his mom had died, he hadn't known how to react. It had been such a long time. He realized then for the first time how much his mom had looked like Lydia. Two years of practice had taught Brandon how to keep his emotions inside, but it was really hard to do. Lydia had wrapped him in a tight embrace and told him how much she loved him and how sorry she was that it had been so long. He had believed her. A month later, his dad's rights had been terminated, he was in jail without bond, and Brandon was settling in with Lydia. For the first time in a very long time, Brandon had felt that life was good.

To Brandon, being with Lydia was a lot like being with his mother. Rachel had loved life and had laughed easily. Lydia was the same way. There was just a joy about her that was contagious. Brandon had found himself relaxing a little and somewhat enjoying things again. There was bitterness, though, that never went away. He wouldn't speak of his dad, and

Lydia wouldn't ask. They had been together for the four years that Brandon was in high school. He had learned how to make friends and had become a social teenager. He had finished high school with honors and several requests from colleges. He had decided to go to a small but distinguished college in California. It had been hard leaving Lydia, but he'd needed a new start away from his past. They had spoken often, and Lydia had learned how to use the computer and internet to help keep in even better communication. This couldn't keep the distance from settling in, especially after Brandon started drinking. He had eventually pulled himself together and graduated at the top of his class with a bachelor's degree in journalism. He had moved back in with Lydia for a short period of time until he had taken the job at the *Journal*. He had relocated to Miami and started working for the Mr. Evans at the small newspaper.

Brandon sat up, swung his legs off the side of the bed, and put his head in his hands. The emotions were just too heavy, and he was feeling them all at once. Pain, disappointment, grief, and anger fought each other in the turmoil. Brandon felt like he was getting ready to explode.

He quickly stood up and tilted his face toward the ceiling like he was facing all of Heaven. He planted his feet and stood his ground. "God, I know that you can't be there. If you were, then I wouldn't have lived a life full of pain. Gram says that you are a god that cares, yet you certainly didn't care for me. You took my mom away and you gave me an alcoholic father with an iron fist. Here's my final offer: If you exist, if you care, then prove it to me. You're going to have to show me where you were when I was in pain and suffering. You must show me what you have ever done for me. That's my final offer. I want proof."

Brandon's words resounded through the corridors of Heaven like a trumpet. Simeon felt the winds of change and expectation flow through his blonde hair. It was time. God looked at His servant and said one word: "Go."

On swift wings, Simeon obeyed. He had delivered God's message to Lydia, and now his assignment was taking him to Brandon. He hoped Lydia's prayers were strong enough. They just had to be. It was the moment to bring an end to Brandon's struggle.

God watched silently for a moment and then said, "So it begins."

Lydia felt the atmosphere in her room change. It was suddenly charged with electricity, nothing she had ever experienced before. Her perception was one of sheer enjoyment and excitement. She was aware of a spiritual wind engulfing her, and she allowed herself to delight in the pleasure. She knew God was with her. She could feel His arms embracing her. It was confirmed. He had heard her prayers, and He was answering. Her cries of desperation turned to songs of praise. She knew that her night of mourning would turn to joy by sunrise.

Brandon also felt the change in the atmosphere, only he didn't feel so great. The bedroom was filled with a heavy, stifling tension. He looked outside, hoping to see an approaching thunderstorm that would explain the sudden change. The sky was clear, but clouds were gathering on the distant horizon. "A storm is brewing," he told himself, startled by his own voice. He couldn't remember the last time he had been afraid of a thunderstorm, but this one had him worried. It was going to be a big one. Trembling, he lay down on his bed and tried to shut out the uncomfortable sensations that filled the room.

CHAPTER 4

Simeon stood beside Brandon's bed, watching as Brandon twitched in his sleep. A storm was raging outside, sending strong winds and heavy rains plummeting to the earth. He knew the time had come to reveal himself, yet he hesitated. So much depended on this night; so much depended on him. With a sigh, he allowed himself to become visible and then leaned over to shake his assignment into consciousness.

Brandon felt someone shaking his arm. In his half-conscious state, he assumed that it was Lydia. "What is it, Gram?" he asked as he pushed himself up off the bed. He couldn't believe that he had actually slept. He remembered being terrified of the strange sensations filling the room. He had gone to bed fully clothed and simply covered himself with the blanket he kept folded on the foot of the bed. Anything else would have been too much trouble, and he had wanted to shut out the sounds of the terrifying thunder. He had fallen into a fitful sleep with horrifying night-mares flitting just beneath the surface of his mind.

"Brandon." The voice didn't belong to Lydia. It was the deep, resonant tone of a man. Someone was in his room.

With a start, Brandon leapt off the bed and turned around. His body pulsed with adrenaline as he turned on the light, revealing a man who looked to be about his own age. The man was wearing a long white tunic with a silver sash tied around his waist. He was tall, much taller than Brandon's own six-foot frame. Thick blonde hair covered his head, and his wide-set dark eyes looked as though they could pierce Brandon's soul. The man's straight nose and solid jaw gave a hint of tenacity and strength, while his stocky build reminded Brandon of an athlete. Brandon's body tensed as he automatically poised for a fight.

"Who are you?" he demanded. Although he tried, Brandon couldn't keep the fear out of his voice. He cringed at the shaky sound emanating from his own throat.

"My name is not important; however, for our time together, you may call me Simeon," came the reply.

"What are you doing here?" countered Brandon. He couldn't explain it, but he was strangely comforted by the man's gentle voice. His heart began to slow its pulsating rhythm and return to normal again.

"It's quite simple, actually. You sent an ultimatum to my Father, asking for proof of His existence. Here

I am." The statement only added to Brandon's confusion.

"If God exists, He has to do a lot better than an intruder in my bedroom. Where's the proof in that? Did my grandmother put you up to this?" Brandon would definitely have to discuss this with Lydia. Scaring him out of his mind was not the way to get her point across. Brandon began to get angry with his grandmother.

Simeon paused before he responded to the question. "Your grandmother has been praying for you for years. Her prayers reached Heaven, and God sent me here to answer them."

Brandon's frustration and anger immediately evaporated in his concern for Lydia. She was alone, and he feared for her safety with a stranger in his home. "Gram! Gram!" he called.

"She can't hear you, Brandon," Simeon cautioned. "She is with our Lord, and all sounds are being kept from reaching her ears. In a sense, we are alone."

This didn't ease Brandon's anxiety. He jerked open his door and ran for Lydia's room. He pulled on the knob, and the bedroom door opened to show Lydia sitting on the floor, singing. She looked content and perfectly fine.

Brandon turned to go back to his room. On further reflection, he turned and reached into the hall closet for his baseball bat. He didn't own a gun, and his cellular phone was in his room, with this man called Simeon. The bat would have to do as a weapon if things got out of hand. He didn't feel threatened, but it was better to be safe, Brandon told himself. He went back into his room, the bat carefully hidden behind him. He would have to convince this unwanted guest to leave.

Brandon found Simeon standing in the same place he had left him in.

"You're lucky that my grandmother is fine."

"I told you she was," Simeon said and smiled. "You can put the bat down. I'm not here to hurt you."

"I'll keep it with me, if you don't mind." Brandon's words dripped with sarcasm. "Although I think it's about time that you tell me who you are and what you are doing in my bedroom—uninvited, I might add—in the middle of the night."

"I've already told you why I'm here. You asked God to prove that He is there. He sent me, and here I am." Hearing Simeon speak of God made Brandon's stomach twist with nervousness. It was almost as if Simeon knew God personally.

"Okay, so how did God send you?" Brandon's tone held more than a touch of cynicism and causticness.

"How else would I have known about your challenge? My Father and I spoke at great length about this plan. Your grandmother has been crying out to God for years over you. Scripture says, 'The eyes of the Lord are over the Righteous, and His ears are open unto their prayers.' God heard Lydia, and He answered. He sent me. But we also knew that there would be stumbling blocks in our path. We knew how you thought, and we knew why. Pain and grief are hard to overcome, and soon, bitterness has a way of taking control of a person's life. This is what has happened to you. We know that you will never be at peace, or walk in freedom, until you face your past and find God. If anything, tonight should show you how far God will go to find even one person who doesn't believe." Simeon finished his speech and became very quiet. The silence made Brandon nervous.

"What do you mean when you say you knew my thoughts?" Brandon didn't like hearing that his thoughts weren't as private as he assumed they were.

"God knows everything. He knows what you are thinking, and He knows about your past. Your mother's death and your father's abuse created the person that you are. But this is not the way God intended you to live. He wants you to be free."

"Excuse me for a moment. I'm clearly not in prison or enslaved. I'm not wealthy, but my apartment is more than adequate. I have a decent job and good friends, and I have a grandmother that loves me. Yeah, I had some tough times in my life, but who doesn't? I am just fine," Brandon finished in a rage.

"I am not speaking of living in financial stability or of physical freedom. What I mean is living in God-given liberation. This is the freedom that your grandmother walks in and your mother lived in. We do not have long. I am here to answer your ultimatum, so let's go."

"Go?" Brandon asked, puzzled. "Where are you taking me? Church? I doubt that you will find a church open in the middle of the night. Plus, I have had my fill of church people for a long time. They don't want to comfort you in your times of grief. All they want to do is quote platitudes and pretend to care while they go about living their own lives, thankful that they aren't the ones suffering."

"No. We are going back to the beginning, your beginning. Come." Simeon waved his arm. The walls of Brandon's bedroom faded away and were replaced by the sterile surroundings of a hospital room. Brandon could see a person on an operating table. Doctors and nurses rushed all around as they tried to accomplish their many tasks simultaneously. He could hear the sounds of surgical equipment. A heart monitor beeped in the background, oxygen machines pumped air into the patient's lungs. A pungent odor of disinfectant filled Brandon's nostrils, and he grimaced against the smell. The atmosphere produced an air of importance and tension. Brandon shivered against the chill in the room. Whatever was going on, it was serious.

Suddenly, a cry rose above the urgent tones of the surgeon. It was the lusty wail of a newborn baby! The doctors and nurses gave a cheer of relief.

"It's a boy," Brandon heard. "And he looks completely healthy. Take him to the pediatric ICU to

make sure there are no effects from his mother's medications." Brandon couldn't make out who was talking. His eyes followed the baby as the nurse took him
through the doors. The rest of the medical team
refocused their attention on the new mother.

Moments before the surgery was over, something
went wrong. The heart monitor screamed that she
had flatlined. Chaos ensued as the doctors and nurses
scrambled to save her life. One person was doing
chest compressions as another was working the
breathing machine. People were screaming orders
and vital statistics at each other.

The fear rose in Brandon's throat. He looked at
Simeon. "See? I told you that God didn't exist. If He
did, then that baby wouldn't be left alone without his
mother!" He looked back at the stressful scene in
front of him. His hands were balled into white-
knuckled fists as he fought to control his emotions.
"Your God is going to let another mother die!" he
spat.

Brandon looked around him. The action had
stopped. The sounds had ceased.

"Is it over?" Did they lose her?" Everything
seemed surreal, frozen in time.

Brandon looked around for Simeon. He was
standing by the mother's head.

"What is going on?"

"Come here," Simeon answered softly. Brandon
reluctantly obeyed, joining Simeon.

"Look at her," Simeon gently demanded.

Brandon swallowed against his nerves and looked at the woman lying on the table. He gasped as he saw the soft features of his own mother. Rachel had been a beautiful woman. Her eyes were closed, and her hair was confined in a surgical cap, but it didn't take away from his recognition. Although it had been fifteen years since he had last seen his mother in anything but a picture, he knew her immediately.

Tears streamed down Brandon's face. For years, he had longed to see his mother again, and here she was. But this wasn't how he had envisioned the reunion. When he imagined it, she was running to him, healthy again, and picking him up in her arms. Her brown eyes would be sparkling as she laughed. Her laughter had always reminded Brandon of tinkling bells. He could still feel how soft her hair felt when it brushed his face as she hugged him goodnight. Brandon knew that, had his mother lived, he would have been several inches taller and much heavier than Rachel's slight frame, but in his imagination, he was still a little boy running into his mom's arms.

With a trembling hand, he reached out and stroked her cheek. She was so cold. It was like the life was completely gone from her. "Please," he begged Simeon, "show me what's going on. I don't understand."

"I know that you don't," Simeon countered. "You think this is all a vivid dream."

Brandon acknowledged his statement with a brief nod. "You're right; this does feel like a dream. But this is my mom. At least let me see what happens to her before I wake up. I don't remember her having another child after me."

In the distance, Brandon saw a glimmer of light enter the room. It was the only movement in the entire scene. He watched as it grew bigger and brighter. He shielded his eyes so he could keep watching this luminescent apparition. His heart stilled as the light stopped beside his mother and disappeared.

In its place was a man. He looked old, but distinguished. He had hair of pure white and a beard to match. He wore a flowing robe that shone like a freshly polished pearl. Golden threads showed at the seams of the garment and made up the sash that was loosely tied around his waist. The man smiled as he looked down on Rachel. Like Brandon had done, the man reached out and gently rubbed his hands down Rachel's face. Brandon jumped as the stranger began to speak.

"Oh Rachel, my child," the man started. Brandon could do nothing but stare at this man. His voice was deep and strong and held the melodious tones of a brass instrument. Brandon could hear the power and authority in the voice, but he also heard restraint, as if the stranger was holding something back.

The man never once looked in Brandon's direction, or in Simeon's. Instead, he kept his focus entirely on Rachel's face. He continued speaking. "It is not your time yet," the man said as tears ran down his wizened face. "How I long for you to be with me. It breaks my heart to leave you here in this world of pain. But your son needs you. You will be with me soon. In the meantime, Brandon will know you and love you, as you will teach him of me. In the time to come, we will be together."

Astounded, Brandon stared at Simeon. "That baby is me?"

Simeon glanced back at the moving display in front of them. He, too, was openly crying.

The man leaned over and gently kissed Rachel's forehead, breathed on her face, and then faded away. The nervous action started up again. Brandon saw a nurse bring around the electric paddles. But before she could use them, the heart monitor began its regular beeping again. Everyone breathed a collective sigh of relief as Rachel's vitals immediately returned to normal, and the surgery was completed.

Simeon turned to Brandon as the surgery suite faded from view and Brandon's bedroom came into focus again. Brandon blinked his eyes rapidly to clear the lingering tears. He eyed Simeon warily. "What just happened? Who was that man?" he asked. It would be nice to believe that what he had seen had truly happened, but Brandon was skeptical. He knew it had been a dream, just an extremely realistic dream. It had to be. Brandon found himself disappointed.

"You've heard your mother and grandmother talk about your difficult birth, and you knew she nearly died. Rachel told you that she could feel God's presence with her, even through the anesthesia. What you saw was God breathing new life into her. He did it for you, Brandon, because He loves you."

Brandon snorted. "He loves me, all right. He gave her back to me only to take her away again twelve years later. Don't get me wrong, I'm grateful to have had her, but if God loved me, she would still be here with me."

"God does love you, and in time, you will see. But now it's time to go elsewhere. Come."

Lydia sat in her floor, content to continue her praises to God. She thought back to the night Brandon was born. She had come so close to losing her precious daughter that night. The nurse had come out and brought her new grandson out for her to see. Lydia had been so happy that he was there and apparently healthy. There had been so much sadness when Rachel had lost her first child two years before. Yet Lydia had known something more was happening that night. Her spirit had been quickened, and she had known she had to pray. She had kissed Brandon's tiny pink cheek, rubbed his downy head, and then asked the nurse where the hospital's chapel was located.

Once inside the dark room, she had sat in a cushioned pew. The chapel was generic, designed to accommodate any faith. She had placed her hands on the pew in front of her and laid her head on them and then begun to plead with God on behalf of her daughter.

"Oh Father, we need a miracle. My girl has fought so hard to have this child. She loves you, and I know that she will love Heaven. Her heart is ready to go, but please don't take her until she gets a chance to know and love her son. I beg you for this gift. But in the example of Your Son—" Her voice broke as she struggled to continue. The next words were extremely difficult to say. "However, not my will, Father, but Yours, be done. We will praise You for whatever decision You make."

As the words left her mouth, Lydia had felt the burden leave her chest. Rachel would be fine for now. Her health would continue to be precarious, but she would have Brandon—for a time, anyway.

CHAPTER 5

Brandon closed his eyes against the spinning sensation in his head as the walls of his room faded a second time. He wondered what he would see when he opened them. He didn't know if he wanted to look. He waited for a few moments and listened to the sounds around him.

He could hear water running, but it wasn't coming from a river or stream. It sounded more like a faucet, as if someone was washing dishes. He could hear a small child laughing, and it made him smile. He couldn't remember ever laughing like that. The child sounded happy. Then he heard a voice that stilled his heart.

He slowly opened his eyes and gasped. This couldn't be real. His mother stood in front of him. He couldn't help but stare at her. He had been correct about hearing water running in a sink. His mother was wearing a wet apron. They had always joked about the way she did the dishes. She couldn't help but splash water all over herself, and she was constantly getting as wet as the things she was washing. He finally tore his eyes away and allowed himself to look around.

He was in a kitchen, one he vaguely remembered. He could tell by the décor that the house was old. Wood paneling covered the walls. The floor had yellow and green linoleum, and the appliances were pale green. There was no microwave, and that alone attested to an earlier year. The refrigerator was covered with crayon drawings of handprints and animals hanging by magnets. Brandon glanced out the window and knew that it was evening. The sun could barely be seen over the horizon.

He could see a small boy, about four years old, sitting at a wooden table. He knew he was the child, yet he could barely believe that he had once been that young. His dark hair nearly covered his eyes, reminiscent of a classic bowl cut. He was wearing a white shirt with trucks embroidered on it and denim jeans. His legs hung freely as he sat there playing with his plastic soldiers while his mother cleaned up from supper. They must have eaten spaghetti, because the child still had traces of it on his face and red streaks down his shirt. Brandon looked closer and smiled as he spied a noodle stuck in the child's hair. Bath time would be coming soon. He remembered playing in a tub with cars, action figures, and dinosaurs. He used to love bath time.

His mother was singing with him. He laughed out loud as he listened to Rachel's antics.

"Sing with me, Brandon. Tell me if I have it right. *Head, shoulders, knees, and toes.*"

Rachel turned from the sink and pointed to a different body part with every word, and none of them was right. She would point to her elbow instead of her head and her ears instead of her shoulders. Each mistake brought peals of laughter from her young son.

"No, Mommy! That's not right," Brandon would say with a giggle. This was a favorite game between the two of them. Rachel would sing different songs and purposely mess up on each one. Brandon would laugh as he corrected her.

Brandon had forgotten these songs and the joy of childhood laughter. When was the last time he had laughed like that? Happy times seemed so distant now. They'd been erased, replaced by grievous memories.

Brandon heard a car pull up to the house and an engine cut off. He watched as Rachel's demeanor became agitated and furtive as she glanced out the window. "Okay, Brandon. It's time for your bath, and then it's time for bed." She took her son's hand and led him from the room. The adult Brandon and Simeon stayed where they were. Brandon listened to the chattering voice of his younger self as he walked farther away. His mother was still playing along with him, but it seemed to be forced, not as happy or as free as before. Luckily, the child didn't notice. Their voices faded away and were replaced by sounds of water running in another room. The front door opened, and Brandon found himself facing his father.

Brandon was aware of intense anger surging through his body. His throat closed, and his fists clenched. He gritted his teeth to regain control. His father was drunk. He could tell by the red eyes and staggering gait. He watched as Robert careened to the refrigerator and began to rummage through its contents. Cheese and eggs fell to the floor but were ignored as Robert slammed the door closed and turned his attention to cabinets.

"Where is it?" Robert slurred. "I know it's in here somewhere." Brandon had no doubt what his dad was looking for. He had lived through this scenario many times. Whiskey held a massive claim on Robert Moore's life, and it wasn't about to let go. Brandon believed that the hold was so strong, Robert would have sold his own soul for another shot of the fiery drink. In a way, he had. He had sold not only his but Brandon's as well.

"Rachel!" Robert yelled. Brandon's body automatically tensed. He remembered all too well what that tone of voice implied, and he had reacted subconsciously. He listened nervously for his mother to come back into the room.

Rachel appeared in the doorway, her eyes darting from Robert to the open cabinets to the food spilled on the floor and back to Robert. She licked her lips in an anxious habit. Brandon could sense her nervousness.

"Hello, Robert. How was work today? I'm sorry you missed Brandon. He is already bathed and in bed." She cautiously gauged his reaction before continuing. "We had spaghetti tonight. I saved you a plate. Would you like me to get it for you?" Rachel moved toward the stove and opened the oven door. On the rack was a plate wrapped in tinfoil. She pulled it out and began to uncover it.

Even in his drunken state, Robert was faster than his wife. His arm shot out, and the dish flew from her hands. It bounced off the counter, spilling its contents before hitting the floor and shattering.

"Now look what you've done! You're nothing but a clumsy fool," Robert bellowed. "Clean it up and fix me something to eat, woman!"

Rachel reluctantly grabbed some paper towels and bent to pick up the upset food. Brandon could see the tears on her face but saw also that she was in control. Her lips were moving, and Brandon assumed she was praying. Once the spaghetti was soaked up and the shards of glass swept and thrown in the trash, Rachel walked toward the refrigerator and began to clean the mess there, replacing the cheese and wiping up the broken eggs.

Brandon was indignant. "He should clean his own mess!" he exclaimed. "Why should he come home drunk, tear things up, and then force my mother to fix things? Where is your God? Why doesn't he stop this?"

Simeon just turned away from Brandon and focused on the sight before them. The floor was once again spotless, and Rachel was fixing a sandwich and a can of soup for her husband. Things were quiet now and almost appeared normal.

"The man that showed up in the hospital room, where is He now? I don't see a beam of light. I don't see Him. Has He forgotten her already? Is this the God she serves?" Brandon was beyond irritated. He had dismissed his idea that God didn't exist. Now he knew that God cared only when it was convenient for Him.

Simeon turned his sympathetic eyes toward Brandon. "I know what you are thinking, and you are wrong," he commented quietly. "God told me," he said, answering Brandon's questioning look. "He is omniscient, whereas I am not. I only know what is revealed to me."

"Isn't that convenient!" Brandon was trembling with frustration. He knew that the quiet he was seeing now with his father was just a temporary state. After a while, Robert would explode, hurting anyone who happened to be nearby. Brandon was desperately afraid for his mother. His hands clenched and unclenched in useless agitation.

"Where's my bottle, Rae?" Robert demanded, his tone deceptively quiet. Rachel's back straightened. It was clear that she was afraid to answer.

"Robert, I told you that I can't have alcohol in the same house as my son. What would happen if Brandon found it?" Rachel failed at keeping the tremor out of her voice.

"I see," Robert said. He stood and started to walk out of the room. Then without warning, he spun on his heels, hands open, and reached for Rachel's neck.

At that moment, Brandon winced as a shaft of light coursed through the room. It was blinding, and he raised his hand to protect his eyes. When the light faded, Brandon looked again at the picture in front of him.

He expected to see his father holding his mom by the neck. The same move had been done to him many times. In his mind, he assumed he would see his mother crying as his dad worked his sadistic magic on her. Instead, he saw his father's wrist being held firmly in the grasp of the man in flowing robes from the surgical room.

Anger shot from His eyes as He looked at Robert and said, "Not this time, my son. You have hurt my daughter too many times. I beg of you to turn to me and quit running. But you will not harm my beloved child again!"

Brandon looked from his mother to his father, wondering what their reactions were to this interruption. Surprisingly, they both seemed unaware of this stranger in their midst. Rachel was crying, but there was peace in her eyes. Cursing, Robert turned and ran out the door. Brandon could hear the car door slamming and tires screeching as his father sped away from the house. He watched as Rachel pulled a chair away from the table and eased herself into it, lowering her head into her hands.

She sat there silently for a moment, and then Brandon heard her praying. Her words amazed him as she thanked God for His protection, and then she prayed for her husband. This sent a wave of bewilderment pouring over her son.

"Why is she praying for my dad? He could have just killed her! His wrath has no limits, especially when he's full of booze!"

Simeon smiled. "Rachel is a true child of God, Brandon. God told His people to pray for those who hurt them. Rachel knows that Robert is a lost child. You even heard him called son. God loves everyone. And He will go to great lengths to find one who needs him. Look at what He is doing tonight with us. Rachel is praying that Robert will one day accept God's unconditional love."

Brandon digested Simeon's words. He didn't know how to respond to what he was hearing. His thoughts were interrupted by a small voice as he watched himself as a child enter the room. The young boy stood in the doorway, looking apprehensively at his mother. "Mommy?" he asked. Brandon heard the anxiety in the child's voice.

Rachel opened her eyes and looked at her son. "What is it Brandon-Bug?" Rachel spoke with such tenderness as she reached for her young son that a surge of love and longing crested over Brandon. He reached over to her and tried to brush a strand of hair from her face. She couldn't feel the movement or the touch of his fingers.

Brandon thought the crushing disappointment was more than he could bear. He turned away. "Simeon, I miss her so much. You have taken me to two places now, trying to prove that God is real. The only thing that you have succeeded in doing is proving that God is malicious and likes to cause pain on innocent people. Why else would He have taken my mother? Was He punishing me for not turning to Him? Why else would He force me to remember these things that I have tried to forget?"

Simeon took Brandon's arm and guided him back to the table, where Rachel was rocking the young boy. She was singing softly to him. Brandon leaned in to hear her words.

"Yes, Jesus loves me, the Bible tells me so," she finished. "Brandon, Mommy loves you. One day, though, Mommy will have to leave you. I know you don't understand what I am saying, but you will. But when you wake up that first morning after I am gone, I want you to do me a favor. Remember that I am in Heaven, I will be happy, and I won't be sick anymore. But will you please blow me a kiss?" Rachel choked against her own sobs. "Remember something else. Jesus loves you more than I ever can. He will take care of you, and He will make sure that you will be just fine. Will you remember that?" The little boy nodded against his mother's chest. At his young age, he couldn't comprehend the full meaning of his mother's words.

Simeon and Brandon watched as Rachel kissed the top of her child's head and stood up. She placed him back in the chair and walked to the phone. Brandon reached out to his mother again, but she was fading away. So were the little boy and the outdated kitchen. Brandon's hand touched nothing but air as he found himself standing in his bedroom again. He dropped to the bed as his weeping overtook him and sobs convulsed his body.

Lydia could hear Brandon's cries through the paper-thin walls of the apartment. She started to rise and go to him but felt a check in her spirit. She heard a small voice in her ear saying, "Dear child, wait. He is in my hands, and I will comfort him. Pray. His hour has not yet come but it is drawing close. Remember where I have already brought him from."

Lydia desperately wanted to console her grandson, but she had heard from God, and she would obey. Her mind drifted again to the past. She recalled the night she had received the call that would bring Rachel and Brandon home to her.

It had been nearing 10:00 p.m. when the ringing of the phone had broken the stillness of the evening. Lydia was still awake, having never been one to retire to bed early. It was Rachel's voice on the other end.

Lydia had known for several years that this day would come, and she prayed that she would be ready. Robert had gone too far and Rachel wasn't safe anymore. She had spoken tersely and briefly to her daughter. After replacing the phone on its receiver, she had quickly gone to the linen closet for fresh sheets. Lydia could do nothing for a broken heart, but she could give her only daughter and grandson a comfortable bed. Tomorrow, they would work to find a solution, but for tonight, rest was the answer.

Rachel and Brandon had arrived about an hour later, Rachel carrying Brandon inside. He had fallen asleep and she didn't want to wake him. Lydia could still see the teardrops that clung to his eyelashes, and her heart wrenched at the sight. Rachel, too, had been crying, but Lydia could see the inner peace that comes only from God. They hadn't spoken. They hadn't needed to. Rachel and Brandon had slept together in the guest room. None of them had known what the next day would bring, but they weren't going to think about it. For that night, anyway, there was safety.

Brandon's sobs dissolved into silent tears and then diminished altogether. Simeon stayed with him and gave some comfort to the broken man. He knew what the night's enterprise was costing Brandon. In a way, he longed for it to be over. He knew, however, to stick to the strategy to achieve the desired outcome.

It was no different than the wars Simeon had fought in the spiritual realm; this was, in fact, yet another battle raging in Brandon's heart that needed to be won. But Brandon needed this time to heal before moving on.

"I remember that night," Brandon started quietly, his voice a mere whisper. "Mom called Gram, and we went to her house. I fell asleep on the way there and slept all night. I didn't even wake when my mom carried me inside. I was so scared the next morning because I didn't recognize where I was at first." Brandon paused as the memories continued to rise to the surface.

"When I saw that both Mom and Gram were there, and my dad wasn't, I was fine. Actually, I think I was relieved, because my dad scared me so much. Mom had tried to put me in bed that night when she heard Dad's car, so I wouldn't know if anything happened. It didn't work. I heard it, and I saw it. I don't think I ever told Mom that I was hiding behind the door that night." He turned to look at Simeon. "Why are you showing me these things? I have tried to bury them for so long, and now you are dredging them again."

"There are things that you must see, in order for you to heal, and to trust, again. I think that you will feel easier about this next one, though. Come, let's go to the woods."

CHAPTER 6

Brandon's mind reeled with the thought of yet another place and time from his past. He hoped this one would not be as emotionally turbulent. Trees began to appear from nowhere, surrounding him. They were tall; Brandon could barely see the sky above them. He noticed the chill in the air, and he knew that night was approaching. From the distance, he heard the sound of laughter. He looked for Simeon, but he wasn't there. He felt abandoned.

Brandon sat on a fallen log, waiting. It wasn't long before he saw himself, as an eight-year-old child, ambling toward him through the dense forest. He had grown a lot in the passing years. He smiled when he noted his hair. The longer, shaggy hair from earlier was gone, and in its place was a neat and tidy crew cut. He liked the improvement.

The child was carrying a homemade sword. It was a long stick with duct tape on one end. On his head sat a pot, representing a knight's helmet. He was locked in play as he fought an imaginary dragon.

Brandon remembered these romps through the woods. He and Rachel were still living with Lydia. Rachel's health was too precarious for them to live alone. The constant doctor visits and hospital stays required someone to be with Brandon in his mother's absence. Lydia's house was adjacent to the woods, and he loved to play in them. These trees had been his haven, a place to shut the world out and let it be whatever he created. He had thoroughly enjoyed pretending to be a soldier, a knight, an animal, whatever his fancy was at the moment. Even at this young age, Brandon could spin a story, and it was evident in his imaginary play.

The young Brandon walked through the woods, oblivious to the growing darkness. He slashed his sword at the dragon, conquered the heart of the maiden, and won the kingdom from the evil ruler. He was in his element as he worked his charm on the piles of leaves that he tromped through. To him, they weren't leaves but tiny people from an enchanted land.

"I'm sorry," the child said as Brandon watched in awe. These times of imaginary play had eluded his memory for quite some time. "I have just defeated the dragon-lizard. I must pass through your village to claim my reward. Please forgive me if I step on you." Then he laughed as the wind blew the fallen leaves in a whirlwind around him and he dropped his sword and ran joyously through them. The sound of a night owl echoed on the wind, and young Brandon jumped as he became cognizant of the time. Reality broke through the imaginary world. It was nearly dark, and he was lost.

In an instant, the scenery changed, and Brandon was no longer in the woods. Instead, he was inside of Lydia's house. He could see Rachel standing at the door, looking out toward the backyard, watching for her little boy. Worry had taken the color from her face and left an unhealthy pallor. "Where is he, Mom? It's not like him to stay out this late." Her voice was filled with desperation, and she was wringing her hands anxiously. "It's supposed to rain tonight, and he didn't take his jacket. What are we going to do?"

Brandon watched as Lydia fought to control her emotions. She chewed on her lower lip as she looked at Rachel, and Brandon could tell that his grand-mother's concern was as much for her daughter as it was for her lost grandson. Rachel had a swollen appearance. The lupus required daily injections of steroids, the side effects being fluid retention. She was limping as pain settled in the joints of her knees and ankles.

"Sit down, Rachel. You can't get worked up like this. You're going to make yourself sick, and that won't do Brandon any good."

Brandon breathed a sigh of relief as Rachel did as she was told. She sat, remaining fidgety, rubbing her knees with her hands. "Okay, Mom. I'll stay calm.

Now what?" She waited breathlessly to hear Lydia's advice.

"First of all, we call the police. I'm sure they will search the area for a lost little boy. In the meantime, and more importantly, we pray. Brandon is lost to us, not to God. He knows where your son is, and He knows where to lead us." Lydia rose from the couch and picked up the phone to place it in Rachel's trembling hands. Rachel started dialing, hit the wrong number, hung up, and dialed again.

"Hello? I need to report a missing child. He's eight; he's my son," Her voice broke into sobs as her mother took the receiver from her. Lydia quietly gave the dispatcher the address and gently laid the phone back in its cradle. She walked back to her daughter, knelt on the floor in front of her, and took Rachel's hands into her own.

"Oh Father, creator of our universe, hear our cries tonight. There is a precious little boy out there that is lost from our sight, but not from Yours. Lord, we ask for Your divine intervention. Be with Brandon. Keep him safe, warm, and dry. Send your angels to guide him and show him the way back to our arms. We ask this in the name of Your Son, Jesus. Amen."

Immediately, Brandon was taken back to the woods. He could see the child, crying, huddled beside a tree. The wind and the leaves that had been his friends and playmates only moments before were now his enemy as they moved and danced to their own music. The shadows lengthened and grew darker. He trembled in the cold as he called out for his mother.

Brandon looked again for Simeon. He felt as alone as the young boy in front of him appeared to be. He could remember it now—the solitude, the noises, the piercing cold—all of them were cemented into his recollection. After the terror of this night, he had avoided the woods for a year.

The other events that the adult Brandon had relived this night caused him to look around for evidence of God in this moment. He assumed that because Simeon had left him alone, God wouldn't come this time either. Had they decided that Brandon wasn't worth their thoughts and efforts? The emptiness was intolerable.

He sat down beside the child, huddling in the trees, and trying to remember how he had been rescued. He wanted to console the boy, but he couldn't. Brandon though that, maybe if he just stayed with the boy, neither one of them would feel so alone.

The gripping silence was broken by the child as he voiced one word: "Jesus."

Brandon felt the wind being sucked out of his lungs. Had he said that? He must have heard it from Rachel. He was amazed to hear himself praying as a child. He didn't remember ever doing that. As he stared at the child, warmth began to spread over his body. The boy felt it, too, Brandon could tell; his shivering was slowing. The young Brandon was looking around to see where it was coming from. The adult Brandon couldn't help himself; he looked too.

Simeon appeared next to the child, and he wasn't alone, Brandon noticed. There was another man with him. Brandon immediately recognized God. The two of them were creating a shield over the boy to keep him warm.

Brandon watched as, after a few minutes, Simeon tugged at the child's arm. "Get up," Simeon softly whispered in the boy's ear. "Go this way." He turned the boy to the left and then followed, with God, as young Brandon walked away. The three of them disappeared as the adult Brandon was left cold and alone once more. In the distance, Brandon heard loud shouts as men from the search party caught sight of the boy. He closed his eyes as he remembered the relief he had felt when he had heard them as a child. He had been found, and he was going home.

He listened, eyes still closed, as the joyous exclamations faded away. When he opened his eyes, he was in his grandmother's house. His mother was crying as she held her young son in a tight embrace, but this time, her tears were happy ones.

"Thank You, Lord," she kept repeating. Lydia informed Rachel that she had fixed Brandon a warm bath. She knew that the heat from the water would warm the child as well as clean and relax his body. Rachel whispered, "Thank you, Mom," as she carried Brandon to the bathroom.

Brandon watched them leave, unnerved by the feelings of nostalgia washing over him. He jumped when he heard Simeon's voice breaking the silence. "Now you know how you got home."

"Where have you been?" he demanded.

Simeon wasn't insulted by the question. "I've been near. But you needed to face this one alone, as you experienced it that night. I was watching you, just as I was there to lead you to the search party. You saw me, and you saw God. Many times, people feel like they are in solitude when, in fact, they are surrounded with love and prayers. Human eyes are veiled; they cannot see in the spirit realm unless that curtain is removed. Tonight, God has taken away the veil over your eyes and allowed you to see clearly how things have worked in your favor. Not every memory is pleasant, and even now, you may not be able to discern the good from the bad, but God was there, and God is here."

Brandon scanned the room for the man he had seen previously. He was nowhere to be found. "I thought you said God was here. I don't see Him," protested Brandon, although he was relieved. His image evoked feelings that Brandon wasn't ready to encounter.

"He is allowing you to see some things, but you still cannot see everything. God is not always in human form." Brandon and Simeon began to walk toward the door and down a narrow hallway that led into a bedroom.

"This was my room. I remember these fireman sheets. I had them when I was younger. There was a time that I wanted to grow up to be a firefighter."

Rachel lay beside her son on Brandon's bed. The boy's hair was still damp from his bath. Rachel gripped him in desperation like she never wanted to let go. "You scared me tonight, Brandon, but God took care of you," she wheezed. Brandon recognized the labored breathing that Rachel had endured the last few years of her life. "I prayed for Him to send His angels to show you where to go."

"I'm sorry, Mom. I was playing, and I wasn't paying attention. I didn't know it was getting late. I won't do it again, I promise." The child paused before confessing, "I prayed too," in a whisper. "I was so scared, and I was cold. I didn't know how to get home. Then I remembered what you said about Jesus helping people. So I said 'Jesus.' Guess what happened?"

Rachel was listening with undivided attention. She was enthralled by her son's story. "What?"

"All of the sudden, I felt warm. It was almost like someone put a blanket on me, but I didn't see anyone. Then I heard someone talking to me. Only it wasn't in my ears; it was in my head. He told me to start walking. I did, and that's when I saw all the people."

Moments later, young Brandon was asleep in his mother's arms. Rachel, too, drifted off to sleep. Brandon remembered waking the next morning to find her still with him. Her relief at having her son home had left her incapable of leaving him during the night. He treasured the feeling of contentment and love that seeing her next to him had given him. He had never completely forgotten it; it was just hidden until it was presented to him in this manner.

Simeon tugged on Brandon's arm. "It's time to go. We are going to church."

Lydia sat in the overstuffed chair, cradling her Bible in her hands. She was tired, but she knew the night was far from over. The Lord was revealing things, all involving Brandon, and she knew that when this ordeal was over, he would be a new person, a soldier in Christ's army.

She smiled, remembering the way Brandon would play in the woods behind her house. He was never alone as long as he had his imagination. That child could create a magical place in such a way that Rachel and Lydia were awestruck. They had known that he was a talented boy and would do well with a writing career. Brandon was already successful at the *Journal*. In the few years he had worked there, other papers had made him offers, but Brandon had turned them all down. He knew where he was supposed to be.

Her mind drifted to the night when Brandon's preoccupation had gotten him lost. Rachel had been consumed with worry and fear. Lydia had also been scared and anxious, but she'd had to hide it from her daughter. If Rachel had known, she would completely fall apart. Lydia had to be strong for both of them.

After the police arrived at the house, they had asked a lot of questions. At first, they had thought maybe Robert had taken Brandon. Eventually, Robert had been found, intoxicated, at a nearby bar. The employees had said he had been there all evening, ruling out parental kidnapping. A search party had been formed, and they had begun to comb the woods looking for Brandon. Lydia would never forget the feeling of awe and appreciation as she stood on her back porch, watching the volunteers waiting for instructions from the sheriff. Her God was faithful, she had known, and He would bring Brandon home.

As night had continued to fall, the darkness had become a forceful enemy. There was a cold front moving in, and the temperature was dropping drastically. There was moisture in the air, signaling that rain was on the way. Silently, Lydia had prayed for the clear weather to hold until Brandon had been found.

After what seemed like an eternity, they had heard a shout coming from the woods and known the rescuers had been successful. Rachel had rushed to the door and taken Brandon in her arms just as they had carried him up the porch steps. Their prayers had been answered.

Lydia had run some warm water in the bathtub, offering Rachel precious time with her son. She could feel herself decompressing and needed to keep busy. Much later, as Brandon and Rachel had lain on his bed, talking and then finally succumbing to sleep, she had stood outside the bedroom door and listened.

Rachel had barely been able to breathe, a strong indication that the lupus was gaining its hold. Lydia wouldn't be surprised if another hospital visit was imminent. She had leaned on the doorframe as she struggled to keep her tears in check as she realized that the task was daunting and she was failing. She had allowed her trembling legs to carry her to her own bedroom. Quietly, she had knelt on the floor as she surrendered to her anguish. She had carried her thanks, love, and distress to God. As always, she had been met with open arms and had relished them as they took her burdens to Him. That was the God she served. That was the God Who was chasing Brandon.

CHAPTER 7

Brandon heard singing in the distance. As it drew closer, he could make out the familiar words of "Great Is Thy Faithfulness." He knew he was at Lydia's church even before it came into complete focus. The small white building with its wooden steeple was unmistakable. He remembered the stories of how his grandfather had built the steeple and bought the bell for it just before he died. In fact, it had rung its first chord at his funeral. Lydia had been a widow since Rachel was a teenager, but she had loved her husband with all her heart and never remarried.

Brandon and Simeon entered the church. Brandon recalled the padded pews perched on the worn red carpet. The congregation was mostly elderly people and young children. He remembered how friendly everyone was and how much they seemed to care.

The choir finished the hymn, and the pastor stood to receive prayer requests. Brandon could see Lydia sitting on the right side of the church, near the front. An eight-year-old Brandon sat quietly beside her.

"This is a few days after you were lost in the woods," Simeon explained. Brandon remembered how rough those days had been. Rachel had become extremely ill the day after the incident. Lydia had finally convinced her to go to the hospital's emergency facilities, and she had immediately been admitted.

Brandon heard his young voice speak up. "Please pray for my mama. She's sick. I want her to get better and come home."

The pastor gave a sympathetic smile as he looked at Brandon, and then turned his gaze toward Lydia. "Will you give us an update on Rachel?" he asked her.

Lydia cleared her throat and was quiet for just a moment. "She's doing some better. They are adjusting her medications. The steroids have been increased temporarily, and they are worried about blood clots. She has developed them in her legs in the past, so they have put her on a blood thinner. If one forms and breaks loose, there is the risk it of going to her heart." Lydia stopped for a moment to regain her poise. "If she continues to improve, though, she will be released later this week. Please continue to pray for her. She needs them, as do Brandon and I." Her voice broke, and the pastor began to pray.

"I remember that morning," Brandon started. "Mom was starting to feel a little better. Her breathing was more relaxed, and they said that she could come back home soon. I knew that God was going to heal her, but instead, He took her away. I can never forgive Him for that."

Simeon wasn't surprised at the words, or the vehemence behind them. He had heard many people blame God in their grief. God took it all without malice, because He could see the bigger picture, whereas man couldn't. God also understood man's emotions, which were constantly changing. Simeon knew that Brandon didn't comprehend this yet but would once he realized God's love for him.

Brandon turned his back on the pastor, indicating his unwillingness to hear what the man was saying. He wanted no part of a god who caused pain instead of taking it away.

The pastor's words filled his ears, despite Brandon's attempts at blocking them. "Lord," the pastor prayed, "we know that you have a special plan for your daughter Rachel. It breaks our hearts to see her suffering, and we know it breaks Yours as well. Your own Son was sent to earth to bring healing, both spiritually and physically. The stripes on His back are proof that He has the power to heal, but help us to understand that healing comes in several ways and in different forms. Help us to understand that Your will and Your plan may not be the same as ours. And we will honor You, no matter the decision."

The pastor continued to pray for other requests, but Brandon could no longer hear him. Instead, he was hearing the echo of the pastor's prayer in his ears. "What did he mean by 'Your will and Your plan'?" he asked Simeon.

"He meant that sometimes God decides to heal by bringing His child home. Heaven is the ultimate healing because there is no illness, no sadness there. Only praising God and living in true love await us when we reach our final home with God."

Brandon tried to absorb Simeon's words. He liked the idea of his mother no longer hurting, yet he still rejected the idea that God wouldn't heal her and leave her with him, her son. And his mind had rallied against Heaven so long that it was hard for him to fathom that it was actually a place of true peace.

He continued to observe the service. His focus was mainly on Lydia, as she tended to the younger him. The child Brandon was growing restless, and she pulled a coloring book and crayons from her large purse and handed them to him. He settled down immediately as he began to draw. Brandon contemplated the child more closely. The boy who sat next to his grandmother bore little resemblance to the man he was now. Physically, he the same person, but the child held on to hope; it was evident in the look he bore on his face. He retained an innocence that had disappeared as he had grown. Now, Brandon found that he missed it.

The church faded and was replaced with another bedroom. He was in Rachel's bedroom. She was lying in bed, wrapped in a bathrobe, not quite asleep. Her breathing was still labored, but not as bad as it had been the night Brandon was lost. She frequently gave in to spasms of coughing that left her winded and exhausted. Her hair was pulled back from her face, revealing a rash that covered both cheeks. Her entire body was swollen, making her legs and ankles puffy, and she was bruised all over as though someone had taken a baseball bat to her. Brandon nearly cried at the sight.

"When is this?" he asked Simeon.

"This is a few days after the church service. As you can see, God answered your prayer and she came home from the hospital. She's resting, but she's waiting for you to come home and tell her about your day at school." As Simeon spoke, Brandon could hear a commotion down the hall. He watched as the door was flung open and his younger self came running in. He saw himself jump on the bed and flop down next to his mother.

"Mom! You're home. This is the best day ever!" The child was overjoyed with his mother's presence, and his enthusiasm couldn't be contained. He was bouncing up and down in his excitement.

She turned and smiled at him. "School must have been good today," she said. "You look happy."

"Guess what, Mom?" he answered, and then continued without even pausing. "I won the spelling bee!

I was first out of the whole school! I even beat the older kids! It was so cool."

"That's great. I am so proud of you," Rachel told her son. He gave her a hug.

"Gram said she is going to make me a cake to celebrate. She asked what kind I wanted. My favorite is chocolate. But I asked for strawberry 'cause I know it's your favorite. We can celebrate your homecoming too! Is that okay?"

Rachel choked back tears. She loved this son of hers with every fiber of her being. "That would be great," she managed to say. "I'm feeling better, so maybe I can come eat with you and Gram at the table tonight. I'm tired of eating in bed, and hospital food is gross."

The boy grinned at his mother. "Mom, I said, 'Thank You,' to Jesus today for bringing you home. I really missed you." He stopped for a minute, and then he sobered. "Will you go away again? I don't want you to."

Rachel sighed as she understood that the time had come to tell her son what she knew. "Brandon, I am very sick. The doctors are doing everything they can, but it's not working. God has been taking care of me, and He is letting me love you for now. One day, He is going to take me to Heaven. He will take care of you, and Gram will still be here."

Brandon started crying. "I don't want you to go!" The thought of life without his mother was unbearable.

"I don't want to leave you either, but my body is getting tired. It wants to get better, and it just can't. When I go to Heaven, I won't hurt any more. It won't be hard to breathe any more either, because people don't get sick there. There won't be any medicines to take, and I won't have to give myself those yucky shots again. Heaven is going to be beautiful, and I will be there, waiting for you to come be with me."

The young Brandon was openly sobbing now, and the older one wasn't doing much better. This conversation had been hard enough the first time. The child started speaking again. "But I don't know how to get there. Is it far away?"

"Yes and no. You can't get to Heaven with a car or an airplane, so in that way, yes, it is far away, but God makes Heaven close. That is how you get there, by believing in Jesus and asking Him to come into your heart. Then, one day, we will be together again."

"How do I do that?"

"Do you remember the stories that you heard in Sunday school, about Jesus and the cross?" Rachel asked.

"Yes." The little boy was clinging on to every word Rachel spoke.

"You just pray and tell God that you are thankful that Jesus died on the cross for you. You ask Him to forgive you for the things that you have done wrong, and you ask Him to live in your heart. After that, you live the way God wants you to, and pray every day.

Then, when your life is finished, you will come to Heaven."

"Can I do that now? Because we don't go to church for a long time, since it's only Tuesday and church isn't until Sunday."

Rachel giggled. "No, silly. You don't have to be at church to pray. You can pray wherever and whenever you want to. You can pray right now if you want to."

Brandon hesitated, and then he asked, "Mom, will you pray with me?"

The room became dark as time was suspended, but a strange light surrounded Rachel and her son. The light was now familiar, and Brandon could once again see God. He was sitting with them on the bed and wrapped His arms around them as they prayed. God seemed to be crying, but He was also smiling, so they must have been tears of joy. Brandon could hear strains of beautiful music in the background. He looked at Simeon with questioning eyes.

"Angels don't know what redemption feels like. That is a gift only for man. But we rejoice when someone gives his heart to our Father. We sing songs of praise and celebration. You were getting ready to celebrate a victory at school and Rachel's homecoming from the hospital, and we were celebrating your homecoming to us that day."

Brandon thought about a heavenly celebration as Rachel's room faded from view.

Jennifer Wade

Lydia closed her Bible and leaned her head against the cushioned back of the chair. She remembered bringing Rachel home from the hospital several days after Brandon's incident in the woods. Rachel had been terribly sick. Lydia had known that Rachel would be leaving her. She had prayed and asked God to intervene, but when she hadn't felt at peace about her prayer, she had asked God for strength to face the inevitable.

Brandon had been in school that day when Lydia had brought Rachel into the house. He had come home and been so excited because he had won the school spelling bee, beating children several years older than himself. In addition to that, his mom was home, and suddenly it was like Christmas morning for the child. Lydia had offered to bake a cake to celebrate. She hadn't been surprised when he had asked for Rachel's favorite, strawberry. Lydia couldn't tell him that Rachel probably wouldn't be able to eat it. The lupus and the attack and prescriptions had left sores all over the inside of her mouth. Lydia had made chicken and dumplings for dinner, knowing that the milky substance would be easier for Rachel to eat.

She had set the table and gotten the food ready while Brandon spent time with his mom. They would be coming down momentarily. Lydia spent the time praying for her family. "Lord, be with me and Brandon. I've lost my husband; I can't bear the thought of losing my daughter. And Brandon needs his mom, he

72

is so young. Rachel will need Your strength as these days pass way too quickly for all of us. Wrap us in Your love. Let this time be full of joy and not pain."

Brandon had raced down the hall and burst into the kitchen, his face red. Lydia knew he had been crying. He had flung his arms around Lydia, and she had held him close.

He had sat there for a moment before he spoke. "Mom told me that she would have to leave one day. She said that she was going to Heaven. I'm going to miss her, but she said that you would take care of me. She also said that I could go to Heaven one day and be with her again. I prayed. Jesus came into my heart. I'm happy about that. But I'm sad about my mom."

His eyes had filled with fresh tears as he had buried his face against Lydia. He had clung to her as much as she had clung to him. Together, they had cried as they imagined the years they would spend without Rachel.

Lydia's thoughts returned to the present. Tears streamed from her eyes at the painful memory.

"God, why are you reminding me of these things now? How can they help my grandson?" She waited for the answer that she knew would come.

"Peace, my child. Brandon must remember, and so these things must happen. But they will be for my glory. Watch, wait, and pray. Your joy will return."

"Yes, Lord. I hear. I will obey." Lydia returned to her prayer with renewed fervor.

CHAPTER 8

Brandon's eyes focused in the dim light of a hospital room. Rachel was asleep on the bed, and her lungs were working overtime, trying to squeeze each breath out. She had lost all the puffiness from earlier; in its place was a mere shell of the mother he knew. Her hair, once so thick and vibrant, was now dull and thin. Brandon's heart lurched at the sight. He knew what he was about to see, and it made him angry.

"Why have you brought me here?" he asked Simeon through clenched teeth. "Haven't I seen enough? You've proven your point that God was there, but why must I relive this moment?" Brandon didn't want to see this a second time.

Simeon turned his compassionate eyes to Brandon, and then to the door of the room. It was slowly opening. Brandon watched as Lydia slowly walked to Rachel's bedside. She was trembling. Grief and worry had aged her tremendously. Although Lydia's current visit to see him in Florida was several years after this scene had taken place, Brandon thought she looked older here in this hospital room than she had when he had opened the door and seen her standing outside his apartment. That seemed like an eternity ago, even though Brandon knew that only an hour or two had passed since their argument had driven them to their separate bedrooms.

Lydia sat and took Rachel's hand in her own. "I spoke to the doctor, baby. Your tests came back. He was right. The lupus has attacked your lungs and left cancer in its path of destruction."

Rachel slowly opened her eyes. "I'm going home."

"Not this time. I'm so sorry." Lydia couldn't hold her tears any more. The dam exploded, and her shoulders quaked with her weeping.

"No, Mama. I'm going home. Jesus has already told me that my pain is almost over. I just wish that I could see Brandon grow into the fine man that I know he will be. Take care of him. He will need you. I will see him again. God has promised me that. And God is a man of His word." The words were mere whispers as they drained her energy, and soon she was sleeping again.

Lydia was amazed at what she had heard. Rachel knew that she was going home to be with her Lord. Lydia felt an odd mixture of grief and jealously. She selfishly wanted Rachel to stay here with her and

Brandon, but she didn't want her sick any more either.

"Oh Father," she pled, "I don't want to have to walk this road. You gave Your Son for me, and now I have to give my child back to You. I thank you for allowing me to borrow her for a time, but I am finding it so hard to let go and give her back to You. It should be me, not her. I have lived a good life, and Rachel is just beginning hers. Give me the strength to let her go back into Your arms." Lydia laid her head on Rachel's bed and continued to cry as she prayed.

Brandon watched in awe. "My mother wanted to die?" He couldn't believe what he was hearing.

"Rachel didn't want to leave you so soon, but she was ready to go. Her heart was already set on Heaven. Her body just had to catch up."

Brandon looked at Lydia again. God now stood behind her, His hands on her shoulders as she poured her heart out to Him. He too looked at Rachel with love and compassion. He bent low and spoke to Lydia. "I am with you always, even unto the end of the earth. I am with your dear child too. She is treasured by me."

God reached into the flowing robe that He wore, and Brandon watched as He withdrew a small bottle. "Your tears are so precious to me. I will keep them in this bottle and hold them to my heart." The bottle quickly filled, and God capped it and returned it to his tunic. "Go now and get Brandon, for he will need this time with his mother." God faded away, and Lydia stood. She kissed Rachel's forehead and left the room.

Brandon left Simeon's side and walked to his mother's bed. He could see the pallor in her sunken cheeks. He hated seeing her this way, and it was worse this time because he knew what was coming. He looked up as the door opened again. Lydia came back in the room with her arms around Brandon's shoulders.

Brandon was twelve years old now. All traces of the child he had been earlier had been erased. The coming tragedy had caused him to grow up too quickly. His body had matured. A recent growth spurt spoke of his coming teen years. His hair had changed from brown to dark blonde, but his eyes were still a deep brown, almost mahogany. There were red streaks down his face, belying the tears he had already shed.

He seemed nervous. Brandon remembered how it had felt coming into that room, knowing his mother would never walk out of it again. He hadn't known what to say to her, and that had made him uncomfortable. He had wanted to beg her to fight the illness and stay with him. He had wanted to deny what was happening and hide somewhere safe.

Lydia led Brandon to his mother's side. Rachel opened her eyes and smiled when she saw her son. "I love you so much." Each word was a struggle. "I don't want to go, but I can't stay here any longer.

God has a place for me with Him. It's going to be beautiful, and I won't be sick ever again. God is giving me a new body and taking me to a place where lupus and cancer don't exist."

"I don't want you to go. Can't God make you better and let you stay?" Brandon begged his mother.

"He could, but that's not His plan." Rachel looked at Lydia and pointed to the small hospital nightstand next to the bed. Lydia knew what she wanted and reached over to get it. Rachel removed a gold pocket watch from the box and handed it to Brandon. At her instruction, he opened it.

"Life is like this watch. It is always time to be somewhere or do something. In Heaven, there is no real time. The Bible tells us that a thousand years can be like one day for God. So what may seem like a long time here is really only a few hours in Heaven. Whenever you look at this watch, remember that I will see you in a couple of hours."

Rachel's words drifted off. The boy looked at his mother and whispered, "Mama?" Her eyes fluttered open again. "I love you too, and I will see you in a few hours." Rachel weakly smiled as she gave in to sleep. The boy wrapped a tight fist around his new watch as he struggled not to cry. Lydia stepped up and held him closely.

Brandon looked at Simeon. "I still have the watch. I remember those words every time I bring it out. It's in a lockbox in my desk at home. I don't bring it out often, because it hurts too much."

"Life is full of pain. We laugh, we cry, we pray, and we wait. God hears our prayers, and He answers. Sometimes those answers don't come the way we want them to. It's not up to us to know the plan. We are only to trust that God has control and to know that He is the architect in this design of life."

Brandon watched as light filled the room. Suddenly, it was filled with people. They were all dressed like Simeon was, in white robes with sashes around their waists. He looked questioningly at the man that he had come to know as a friend.

"These are my comrades. They are angels, too. You are never alone."

Brandon looked on, amazed at the sight. The angels formed two lines, facing each other. They started at Rachel's bed and continued upward through the ceiling of the room, as if they were standing on a staircase. Down the center of the columns came two men. One was God—Brandon recognized Him immediately. The other, Brandon had never seen before. He had dark wavy hair and eyes that were not quite green but not brown either. They were a beautiful color, and they held such a soft expression that Brandon caught his breath. His skin resembled the tawny hue of an outdoor laborer, and his beard was long and neat.

As the pair approached, the angels bent forward in a bow of adoration. Brandon was intrigued by the sight. He noticed that one angel, near the front, was holding a baby. He glanced at Simeon and was surprised to see him also bowing in deference to the visitors. Brandon couldn't help asking a question. "Who is that baby? What is it doing here?"

Slowly, Simeon and the others rose. If Simeon heard the muttered question, he didn't answer it. Brandon's attention left the baby, and returned to stare at the two men who stood watching Rachel as she struggled to take each breath.

"Who is this man?" Brandon asked quietly. The atmosphere seemed so peaceful that he was afraid to speak above a whisper.

"This is Jesus, God's Son," Simeon answered reverently. Together, they contemplated the events unfolding in silence. After what seemed like an eternity, God looked at His Son and said, "It's time."

Jesus stepped to Rachel, took her hand, and raised it gently. "Daughter, I am here. Come with me."

Rachel's eyes opened, and she lifted her arm. Lydia and the twelve-year-old Brandon marveled at the expression on her face. She looked so happy and so full of peace. She spoke clearly for the first time in days. "Jesus. You're here." Then her eyes closed again. The young Brandon screamed, "NO!" as her hand fell and she stopped breathing. The heart monitor wailed the piercing tone that confirmed what they already knew. Rachel was dead.

Time stood still for the older Brandon too, only this time, he was seeing something different. He looked on as his mother embraced Jesus and then God. She looked happy and healthy. The sickly look from moments before was gone. Rachel looked at Brandon and Lydia as they wept. "May I?" she asked God. He nodded, and she went to their side. She kissed Lydia's head. She leaned in toward Brandon's ears and whispered, "Just a few hours, my child. I will be there, waiting."

Jesus took her hand again and led her to the baby. She laughed with joy as she took it in her arms.

"That's your sister. She would have been two years older than you, had she lived. She has been waiting for her mother to come. Those who are separated on Earth will be reunited in Heaven."

Together, Jesus and Rachel passed through the angels and past the room's ceiling. The angels disappeared with them. It took Brandon a while to notice that God was still lingering in the room with them. He had stayed behind and was holding Brandon and Lydia in His arms. He cried with them as they mourned, but the young boy refused to be comforted. He ran from the room to lament alone.

Lydia stood from the chair. Age stiffened her joints, and the need to move propelled her to stretch her legs. She walked around the room, thinking of Brandon's reasons for being angry at God. She had been through it herself. It had started the day Rachel had died. Lydia had gone to the hospital, knowing her daughter was nearing the end of her life. She had hoped and prayed that she was wrong. The doctors had feared that Rachel's lungs had developed cancer. Upon X-ray, they had found nodules covering the interior of both lungs, and a biopsy had confirmed everyone's suspicions. Lydia had spoken to the doctor for several minutes before leaving him and entering Rachel's room.

She had just looked at her daughter for a minute before disturbing her rest. Then she had taken Rachel's hands and broken the terrible news. Rachel had surprised her by already knowing, even though the doctors hadn't yet told her. She was happy. She wanted to go home to her Lord. Hearing Rachel talk of Heaven had nearly undone Lydia's resolve. She was going to miss her sweet girl. Rachel's father had passed away years before, while Rachel was still in high school. Now Brandon would be all Lydia had left.

She had waited until Rachel had gone back to sleep and then had gone to get Brandon. The child would need this last time with his mother. Maybe Rachel could give Brandon some comfort. He would be so devastated.

Brandon wasn't handling this crisis very well. He had become angry and withdrawn during this hospital stay of his mother's. He had known that Rachel wouldn't be coming home again, and he was scared. He was too young to lose his mother, yet Lydia knew life could be unfair at times.

Brandon had been in the waiting room. The nurses had taken the boy into their care. They had known what was happening and had tried to be friends with him and comfort when they could. They had brought him sandwiches and games while Lydia visited Rachel. After Brandon would come from the room, concluding his time with his mom, he would break down in their arms and cry. They had known that Lydia needed to heal before she could help Brandon, so they had stepped in as much as possible.

Brandon had walked nervously into Rachel's room. Lydia had told him the news from the doctors. He had surmised that this would be the last chance he had to speak with Rachel. Once again, Lydia marveled at the strength and determination emanating from Rachel. She had requested that Lydia get her a pocket watch for Brandon, but Lydia hadn't known why. She had searched the stores for a nice one and then taken it to her daughter. She had listened as Rachel explained the watch's purpose, and she felt peace, even through her breaking heart.

Lydia and Brandon had sat together and watched Rachel sleep. Then the most amazing thing had happened. Rachel had lifted her hand from the bed and opened her eyes. She had been too weak to move much at all for the last few weeks, and Lydia had been amazed at the strength she was witnessing. Rachel's eyes had opened and focused on something that Lydia couldn't see. Sheer joy had filled Rachel's face as she spoke, the words ringing clear and steady. The tight wheezing and fragile tone had disappeared, and a rosy glow had replaced the paleness of Rachel's cheeks.

The words she spoke still brought chills to Lydia every time she recalled them. "Jesus. You're here." Then she was gone. Brandon had cried out as he too had realized that his mother had left them.

The next few moments were the worst of Lydia's life, yet she had felt God's presence even then. She had known He was with her. Brandon, however, couldn't be comforted. He had run from the room, seeking solace elsewhere. He was still running, and he refused to allow himself to stop. He needed God's comfort, but he denied it all the same.

The next few days had been a blur of making final arrangements and receiving visitors. Brandon had stayed in his room, refusing everyone. His friends from school had made cards and his teachers had delivered them, but no one could get inside the wall that he had constructed around his heart and kept carefully guarded.

Rachel had requested a simple service. After the funeral, they had buried her in a beautiful tree-lined cemetery. Her graveside, on the top of a hill, had a wonderful view of God's creation. Lydia knew that Rachel wouldn't care about her surroundings. After all, she was walking streets made of gold. Lydia had known, however, that she and Brandon would need a quiet place to talk to Rachel when they needed to feel close to her again.

When the pastor had closed the graveside service, Brandon had walked alone to the casket and said his good-bye. He hadn't spoken out loud, but Lydia had known what was in his heart; it had been in hers too. He had kissed his rose, lain it down on the casket, and walked to the car without meeting anyone's eyes. Lydia had followed a few moments later, after she had told Rachel how much she was loved and would be missed.

The ride home had been in complete silence. Brandon had gone straight to his room, shutting the door and blocking out the world. Lydia had prayed for guidance. She hadn't known how to help when she was in despair as well. She had sat at her table and poured out her grief to God. She had risen to answer a knock at the door, ready to welcome another guest paying his or her condolences. Her heart had stopped.

Robert Moore had stood on her front porch, a police car behind him. He was there for Brandon.

Brandon and Simeon stood on a hill, looking at Rachel's grave. Brandon was crying, but gone was the weeping from earlier that night. For the first time since Rachel's death, Brandon was feeling peace. His mother was happy. And although he still didn't understand God, he knew that things were different. He was changing. Maybe tonight, he would stop running and truly meet God for the first time. Brandon found himself hoping that he would.

CHAPTER 9

Lydia stood on the porch, looking at Robert. It had been years since she had seen him. The time had not changed him, except to make him older, but she knew that the lines on his face were more from his alcoholic lifestyle than his age. He looked much older than his forty-one years. She could see the outline of his flask just under his jacket, in the pocket of the liner. Anger sparked in his eyes, and she knew that it was carefully restrained. He wouldn't lose control in front of the police.

The past eight years had been peaceful for Lydia's family. Robert had never once tried to convince Rachel to come home to him. He had discarded his son as well. He had never made any attempt to see Brandon until now. Neither Robert nor Rachel had filed for separation or divorce. They were still legally married; they just didn't reside together. Rachel's days had been spent caring for Brandon and fighting the lupus. Robert barely held on to his job at a local machine shop. He had once been a talented machin-ist, but his desire for liquor had destroyed what could have been a promising career.

Lydia glanced nervously at the officer. He seemed fairly young. His short hair hinted at curls, and his thin build was deceptive to those who might attempt to resist him. The officer's name plate read "P. Hig-gins," and he looked decidedly uncomfortable with his current assignment.

With a nod toward the officer, Lydia spoke to Robert. "What do you want? I just buried your wife, my daughter."

Robert sneered. "It's actually quite simple, *Mother* Stevens." He chuckled. "I want my son. You and your daughter have kept him from me long enough. Now that she's gone, I have been assured that I have every right to Brandon. After all, I am the boy's father. You are just his grandmother. My rights are stronger than yours. Where is he?"

Lydia struggled to keep from panicking. Rachel had entrusted her son to Lydia. She couldn't fail her daughter so soon. "He's in his room. He just lost his mother, and he's grieving." Lydia tried to stall. Maybe she could reason with Robert and he would drop this notion. She wasn't so lucky.

"This officer will see to it that the boy comes with me. Now."

Lydia looked toward the officer again. She anx-iously licked her lips. *Father God*, she prayed silently, *please don't let this happen.* Then she spoke to the policeman. "Officer Higgins, can he do this? We haven't heard from this man in eight years. Brandon hasn't seen his father since the night he nearly killed his mother and they moved in with me. Brandon was four years old. He's twelve now, and we just got home from his mother's funeral."

The officer hesitated, giving Lydia a moment of optimism. Then, as fast as it had come, the hope crashed. "I'm sorry, ma'am," the officer started, his voice betraying the compassion he felt, "we don't have any records of Mr. Moore harming your daughter. Did she file a complaint?" Lydia answered with a quiet no. This was a total nightmare. "I'm sorry," the officer continued. "He is the child's father."

Lydia began to cry. The officer spoke again, trying to soothe her and give her a chance to end the confrontation. "Did your daughter assign legal custody of her son to you before she died?"

Lydia was so overcome that she could only shake her head.

The young man stepped up to the doorframe. "I'm so sorry for this," he repeated as he whispered in her ear. For the first time, Peter Higgins hated his job. He had wanted to be a cop for as long as he could remember, but he wanted to help people, not destroy them. The lady's face had gone so pale that he was afraid she would faint. He had been assigned custody issues before, but this one was tearing at him. He could tell that this man had no love for his son or his dead wife. He was using his own child to inflict pain on an innocent woman. She had just lost her daughter, and was now being forced to lose her grandson. Sometimes the law could be a double-edged sword.

Robert pushed past her and yelled for Brandon. The boy, confused at a new voice, tentatively came out of his room and to the front door.

Robert pasted on a fake smile. "Hello, son. I am so glad to see you again. Your mother wouldn't let me visit you, but that's over now. You are going to come and live with me. Go get your things."

Brandon recognized this man. Although it had been a long time, he still dreamed of a man hurting his mother. Now the man who haunted his dreams was standing just a few feet away. Brandon did the only thing he knew to do; he hid behind his grandmother.

"Brandon, go get your things. You are coming with me." Robert spoke more firmly this time. Like his grandmother had moments ago, Brandon looked to the officer for help.

Again, Peter felt hopeless to stop what was coming. He went to Brandon and knelt before him. "Brandon, please understand. This is your father. You have to do what he says." He turned to Robert and Lydia. "I'll take him to his room and help him pack his belongings. That way, you two can try and talk this out. Brandon will need both of you in his life." He put his hand on Brandon's shoulders and led him toward his bedroom. Brandon still had not spoken.

As Officer Higgins took Brandon out of the room, Lydia and Robert stood facing each other in the doorway.

"You're not going to invite me to sit down? Your manners are declining, Lydia," Robert said sarcastically. Lydia had known that Robert was trouble from the first time he had picked Rachel up for a date. She had bit her tongue then, thinking that Rachel would see the truth and the relationship would go no further. She had cautiously expressed her concern when the engagement was announced, hoping Rachel would change her mind, but Rachel wouldn't listen. She had thought she could be a good example and lead Robert to the Lord.

Lydia waved her arm, motioning Robert into the living room. They walked in, and Robert sank irreverently on the sofa. Lydia perched on the edge of her wing-backed chair, like a bird poised for flight. They sat in silence, waiting for Officer Higgins to come back in with Brandon.

After a few moments of tense quiet, Lydia broke the stillness. "Why are you doing this, Robert? You don't want him. You don't love him. Brandon's been here for eight years, and you've never expressed interest in him before. Why now? He's happy here. He just lost his mom; don't take him away from the security and love that he has here. Please. Let him stay."

Robert seemed to consider the thought. "No. He's my son, and it's my turn now. You and Rachel have turned him into a sniveling baby. He needs a man in his life, not a weak woman teaching him to be a sissy."

Lydia was taken aback at Robert's words and tone. "What do you mean, a sniveling baby? Brandon is still a child, and he has lost someone that he deeply loved. At his age, his world revolves around his mother, and she has just been torn out of his life. It's perfectly normal for him to be sad. He has to grieve."

"So what? Life's not fair. The sooner he learns that, the better he will be," came Robert's sarcastic retort. Lydia was stunned. She feared for Brandon living with this seemingly heartless man. She prayed silently for God to intervene. She needed a miracle, in the worst possible way.

In his room, Brandon silently cried while he packed his clothes. Peter Higgins stood helplessly and watched. His heart broke when Brandon finally spoke.

"He hurt my mom, you know. She didn't think that I saw, but I did. He would come home smelling bad, and my mom would get a scared look on her face. Then she would take me upstairs and put me to bed before anything happened."

Peter absorbed the boy's words. He prayed for guidance to help this boy. "I'm sorry that I can't stop this from happening. The law says that unless there is custody granted to your grandmother, you have to do what your dad says. Do you know if your mom ever called the police to tell them about your dad?"

"She didn't. That last night, I hid behind the door. I could see them through the space between the door and the wall. You know, where the hinges are? Dad couldn't walk right. It was like he was sick or something. He had made a mess looking in the refrigerator and cabinets. He knocked the plate out of Mom's hands and then made her fix more food. He asked her where something was. She said she didn't have it. He got so made that he ran at her. He raised his hand like he was going to choke her, but then he stopped. He left, and we came here to stay with Gram. I never saw him again until today."

Peter listened to Brandon's tale with growing horror. Reading between the lines, he believed that Robert may have a drinking problem. The described scene sounded like he may have been in an intoxicated state. Peter decided right then that he had to help Lydia get Brandon back here, where he could be cared for and cherished. He just didn't know how he would do it yet. God would tell him, though, and until then, Peter would continue to pray for this small family that had been ripped apart.

Peter reached into his back pocket for his wallet. "Brandon, this is my card. It has my name and phone number on it. If you ever need anything, day or night, you call me. I'm going to do my best to help you. I think that you need to hide this somewhere so your dad won't find it. It might make him angry. Be careful, and remember that I will help you if you call me."

Brandon put the card in his pocket. He reached into the drawer and pulled out the pocket watch that Rachel had given him the night she died. "My mom gave this to me. Can you keep it for a while? I'm scared to take it to my dad's, and I don't want Gram to know that I don't have it. It might make her too sad." Brandon's wall finally broke. The tears that had been slow but steady now poured from his eyes as he began to shake with sobs.

Peter's own eyes filled with tears as he held the boy. He knew he would do whatever was in his power to help make this child happy again. Until then, he would cover Brandon with his prayers. He knew he would never forget this assignment.

Lydia watched, helpless, as Robert's truck pulled away. Inside the cab sat Brandon, stiff in his effort to be brave. Lydia felt as if part of her heart was in that truck too. She barely heard the young officer tell her how sorry he was. Her mind couldn't process his promises of help and prayers. She closed the door and stumbled back to her living room. She was light-headed, and the room was beginning to spin. She sank to the floor as the last veneer of restraint fell away. She sat there and wailed out her pain. She felt God trying to comfort, but she turned Him away.

"You did this. You could have saved my daughter, but You stripped her out of our lives. The only thing I had left of her was Brandon, and now You've forced him away too. You could have stopped Robert. You could have made a way, and You didn't. Now I'm alone and Brandon will get hurt."

Once again, she felt God's presence.

"Go away."

Being a gentleman, God slipped away quietly. Lydia felt completely alone for the first time in years. It was unnerving and unpleasant, but in her anger and grief, Lydia refused to ask Him to return.

Brandon sat beside the man he knew was his father. He tried not to cry, but his lips quivered all the same. Rachel had taught him to ask God for help, so he sat there in silence and prayed.

God, help me. I'm alone with my dad, and I'm scared. He hurt my mom, so I think that he will hurt me too. I miss Gram already. Will you take care of her? He felt a little better. He knew God was watching both him and Gram.

His dad's voice cut through his thoughts. "What are you doing over there? Crying? No sense in being a baby. You're a man now, and men don't cry. Straighten up. We're almost home."

Robert turned the truck and pulled into a driveway. Brandon looked out the window, and his heart jolted. He knew this place. He had seen it in his dreams. Those dreams had always been scary. He haltingly opened the truck door and stepped out. The lawn was overgrown and unkempt. It desper-

ately needed to be mowed. Brandon turned and followed Robert through the front door. The smell
immediately overpowered his senses. The whole
house smelled of decay and neglect. Brandon had to
force himself not to cover his nose as he looked
around. Dishes with crusted food were piled everywhere. There was green stuff floating in the glasses,
and the floor felt sticky beneath his shoes.

The den was no better. He could see empty beer
cans littering the floor and pizza boxes piled on the
furniture with other takeout bags strewn across the
floor. Stains from frequent spills had ruined the carpet. Brandon kicked his way through the mess and
continued through the house. When he reached the
bathroom, his stomach heaved. This room smelled
worse than all the others. Evidence of refuse and
vomit clung to the toilet and the floor. Brandon
didn't know how he was going to live here.

"I know. The house is a wreck." Robert came up
behind Brandon. "But now that you're here, I'm sure
it will look good again. I trust that you will do a good
job. Where are you going to start?"

Brandon didn't know what to say. He'd had
chores when he was with his mom and Gram, but he
had never been responsible for a mess like this. Even
at its worse, Brandon's bedroom had been fairly simple to clean.

"What? No answer? Fine. Start here in the bathroom." Robert shoved a mop and bucket at Brandon.
"Cleaning supplies are somewhere around here. I'm

sure you can find them. I'll be back later. I'm meeting some friends. Don't wait up. I'll take you to school tomorrow and make sure they know that I'm in charge. Lydia is gone. Just forget her. To you, she no longer exists."

With that, Robert walked out of the house, leaving Brandon alone. Brandon had never been alone before, and it scared him. He looked at the filthy bathroom again and then got to work.

Brandon sat on the hillside next to his mother's grave. He knew Simeon was sitting next to him, but they sat in companionable silence. Brandon was finally dealing with many things in his past, and he needed no interruption.

Brandon remembered when his father had taken him from Lydia. He had heard the knocking at Lydia's door. He had come down the steps to find Robert standing on the porch with a police officer. He had known something was wrong. He could feel it. His father had spoken to him, and then Brandon had gone upstairs with the policeman to pack. He hadn't been able to fathom much of what was going on, but he had understood that he had to go live with his dad.

The officer had been really nice. He had listened and then held Brandon while he cried. He had said he was going to help Brandon, and he had given Brandon his business card. At the time, Brandon had known that God had sent Peter Higgins when Brandon would need him the most. In his anger, Brandon had forgotten that. He had also forgotten the sense of peace that had come over him in his dad's truck when he prayed. At his dad's house, Brandon had been left alone most of the time, and for that, he was thankful. He could pray as much as he wanted to.

The house had been a disaster when Brandon arrived. It had quickly become clear that Robert hadn't really wanted him but simply wanted someone to care for the house. The added bonus for Robert was knowing how badly he had hurt Lydia.

The very first night, Brandon had scrubbed the bathroom until it had shone like the ones in Lydia's home. The smell had improved immediately. Brandon, exhausted from the emotional day and the hard work, had fallen asleep in his old room. He had awakened when his dad had come bursting through the door, drunk. Robert had grabbed Brandon, yelling that the laundry hadn't been done. That night, Robert had smacked Brandon soundly across his face, and Brandon had been too stunned to react. Robert had dropped him back to the bed and stumbled out of room. Brandon had spent the rest of the night asking God to let him return to Lydia. Even with the time that had passed, Brandon could still recall the feelings of serenity that had washed over him. Even through his pain, he had been able to feel God's presence. How could he have forgotten that?

CHAPTER **10**

Brandon didn't need to be taken back to see his past with his father. He knew it by heart. For two years, he had been told that he was worthless, no one cared, and Lydia had forgotten him. At night he would take out the worn business card from Officer Higgins. He would trace the raised letters with his fingers and pray for the officer to come and rescue him.

Simeon stood beside Brandon and directed his gaze to the side. The peaceful cemetery became the dark rooms of Robert's house. Brandon saw his father passed out in the dirty recliner. Looking out the window, he caught a glimpse of himself as a young teenager. The innocence of the child he had been with Rachel and Lydia was gone. In its place was the hardened shell of a boy who had endured too much.

The boy had a look of distrust in his eyes. His clothes were dirty and ill-fitting. The dark hair that graced his head was dirty and hung in his eyes in greasy strings. Overall, Brandon looked like a very unkempt teenager.

"This is the day I won the attendance award at school. It was the same day that my dad put me in the hospital." Brandon blanched at what was about to happen. To feel the pain while it occurred was one thing, but to be an observer was entirely different.

"I had to bring you here. Your belief in God had been steadily declining in the time you lived with your father. This is where you stopped believing altogether." Simeon knew the events that day too. He was dreading this scene as well. He had been unable to stop Robert's actions and prevent Brandon's pain.

The teenager was at the door now. Brandon watched as the boy tentatively opened the door. He took a moment to assess things before approaching his dad. Cautiously, he reached out and laid his hand on Robert's shoulders.

"Dad?" There was no answer, so the boy tried again. "Dad?"

In a rage, Robert leapt from the chair, his belt already in his hand. "You decided to come back home, did you? What did you wake me up for?" he bellowed.

"Dad, I wanted to tell you—"the boy stammered before the first blow reached his back.

"You forgot something this morning, boy."

Brandon could hearken to the words his father was screaming at the child from the echoes in his memory as much from hearing them out loud now.

But now that he was seeing things with his spiritual eyes, he was aware of something else in the room—something that he hadn't seen or felt that afternoon. Robert dropped the belt and resorted to pummeling Brandon with his fists and kicking hard. Ribs were breaking under the vicious blows. This time, though, Brandon saw God, with his arms wrapped tightly around the boy in a full embrace, absorbing every blow.

"Why is He doing that?" Brandon asked, astonished.

"God didn't want you to hurt, so he took the blows for you. Science has a name for this. It's called adrenaline. You are told that when senses are heightened by fear or excitement, the body can't feel pain as much. This is what adrenaline looks like. God was sheltering you."

For a moment, Brandon became almost detached. He remembered the pain, and he remembered the tears. Seeing things through new eyes had a startling effect; he now could visualize where God had been during these times. His heart was softening.

Robert's rage finally petered out. He gave his son one last punch and then grabbed a bottle of whiskey off the nearby side table and emptied it in one gulp. He gave a half laugh as he stared at the boy huddled on the floor. "Guess you won't forget to make your bed again, will you?" he slurred as he staggered back to his recliner and dropped his drunken body into it. After a very short time, he was asleep again.

The boy pushed himself into a sitting position as soon as he heard the drunken snores of the man in the chair. He carefully put his hand around his ribcage. He knew he had a few broken ribs. He had heard them cracking under Robert's steel-toed boots. His head was pounding, and the room was spinning nauseatingly. He slowly stood and reached into his back pocket. He eased his wallet out and opened it, then pulled out a tattered scrap of paper. It read, "Peter Higgins, Deputy," and listed a phone number. The injured boy knew the time had come for him to reach out. The next beating could be his last.

Brandon felt the agony of the moment hit him full force in the face as he heard the strangled words rip from his own throat. "God, you could have stopped this. Where have You been? I want no part of You if this is how You show Your love."

God heard the words and took them hard, but He turned away, tears in His eyes, as He honored Brandon's tortured words. As He left, Simeon came again and led the boy out the door and to the neighbor's house. Then he too vanished from sight.

"Why did God leave?" Brandon asked Simeon. In every circumstance, God had been right there, and His departure now confused Brandon.

"God will not force Himself onto anyone. If you want Him to leave, He will. It is all part of the freedom to choose that God gives to everyone."

Brandon's eyes adjusted as he was quickly moved somewhere else. He was surprised to find himself standing in Lydia's living room. Peter Higgins was sitting on the couch next to Brandon's grandmother, and they were praying for Brandon. After a few moments, they raised their heads and smiled.

"I feel good about court this time," Lydia began. "Something tells me that Brandon is finally coming home."

Peter agreed. "I've been quietly keeping up with Brandon. I am limited as to what I can legally do, but I did find out that he occasionally comes to school with unexplained bruises and the teachers are beginning to take notice. I have also seen where Robert likes to hang out. He has a favorite bar that has a bad reputation with the police department. We are called out frequently to deal with fights and public drunkenness as patrons leave the fine establishment. There have been numerous arrests in the neighborhood for drunk driving, but we've never had dealings with Robert. Apparently, he can hold his liquor well, at least until he gets home. Am I on your list of witnesses?"

"Of course you are. I just hope that this time, you are allowed to testify. The last time, Robert's lawyers objected and misled the judge, but we have a new judge this time. I've heard good things about him. I'm praying for a good outcome."

Their conversation was interrupted when Peter's phone rang. He opened the phone and announced his name to the unknown caller. His face blanched as he listened to the voice on the other end.

"I'm on my way." He snapped the phone closed. He slowly turned to Lydia, fear evident in his eyes. "That was Robert's neighbor. Brandon just went over there. He has been severely beaten."

Lydia paled and, for a moment, reached out to steady herself. She quickly composed herself and waited for him to finish.

"She has called an ambulance, and she has called the police. Brandon was carrying my business card that I gave him the day he left with Robert, so she called me too. I'm going there now. I will keep you informed as much as I can." He drew Lydia into an embrace, much like a son would his mother. Truthfully, Lydia had come to feel like a second mother to him. He knew she was scared and worried about her grandson. He would do everything he could to bring the boy back to her.

Lydia watched as Peter hurried out the door. Slowly, she closed the door behind her and, as many times before, sank to her knees on the soft carpet. She stayed there for several minutes, pouring her worries to God. Then she waited to hear His voice. He spoke, as she had known He would. She rose to her feet and reached for her car keys and purse. She lived in a small town, so there was only one hospital. She would go there and wait. Her decision made, Lydia quickly acted on it and left, locking the door behind her.

Brandon lowered himself to Lydia's couch. "She wasn't there. I was alone for my entire hospital stay.

They told me that no one had access to me so the judge could talk to me without fear of influence from outside sources."

"You didn't see her, but she was there. She never left. Once or twice, a nurse would sneak her into your room when you were sleeping, but as soon as you began to rouse, she would slip out again."

The thought brought a lot of comfort to Brandon. He remembered times when he had just been starting to wake. He had assumed that he had imagined the soft kiss on his forehead just before he could open his eyes. The disappointment that he was alone when he had fully awakened was intense.

When Brandon was ready to leave the hospital, he learned that an emergency hearing had been scheduled. His attorney, appointed by the court, informed him that Lydia had filed for custody several times. He had been both surprised and pleased to find that Officer Higgins was his ride to the courthouse.

Officer Higgins carried most of the conversation while Brandon tried in vain to quiet his nerves. He wondered if his dad would be there, and the thought terrified him. He finally found the courage to ask.

"No, Brandon. Your father is in jail. The judge in the custody case has already spoken to him. Robert was arrested and charged with malicious wounding and felony child abuse. There is no doubt that his rights will be officially terminated today. The only question remaining is whether you will go into foster care or to your grandmother's. Judges usually like to keep family together, so I suspect that you will be sleeping peacefully at Lydia's tonight," Peter explained.

Brandon nodded and then lapsed back into silence. Peter pulled into the parking lot and stopped the car. "You ready?" he asked Brandon and was answered with an indifferent shrug.

They left the car and walked into the courthouse. Peter took Brandon into a private waiting room. He instructed Brandon that the judge would want to speak with him before making his final ruling. Brandon sat down on a chair as Peter went into the courtroom, and he flipped through a magazine that held little interest for him. His stomach twisted with nervous apprehension. He wanted to go home with Lydia, but what if the things that his dad had told him were true? What if Lydia didn't want him?

The door opened, and the bailiff spoke his name. Brandon stood as his stomach did a massive flop. He felt like he was going to be sick, but he followed the man into the judge's chambers. Once in the room, he tried to calm down by taking slow, deep breaths. The desk was solid wood, and the walls were painted a pale cream. There were pictures of mountains and wildlife hanging on the wall. Brandon smiled slightly at a framed photograph sitting on the shelf. In it were a smiling middle-aged man and a young boy. The man's hair was thinning, and what was left on top was blowing in the wind. The boy looked like a younger version of the man, so Brandon speculated that it was his son. The boy was holding up a fish and grinning. The boy was missing his two front teeth, and it made him look very endearing. They were clearly happy and possessed a close relationship. Brandon envied them.

The door opened, and Brandon jumped. The man from the photograph walked in and smiled reassuringly at Brandon. He was a little older than he was in the picture, and his hair had gone from merely thinning to almost completely gone.

"I'm glad I could have this time with you today, Brandon. I've read the report from your doctors. You've suffered some real injuries. I'm sorry about that, but I hope you are feeling better." Brandon found the judge's tone to be very soothing. He unconsciously began to relax. His eyes flitted to the photograph again, a movement that did not go unnoticed by the judge. "That's my son, Trevor. He was seven years old in that picture. He had just caught his first fish. He just turned thirteen and has his first girlfriend."

The judge studied more paperwork and then focused his eyes on Brandon once more. "It seems we have us a problem. Your grandmother has been after the courts for the past two years to convince them to allow you to come and live with her. She claims that your father abused your mother and you weren't safe. The court should have listened, but unfortunately, until now, there was no proof, only allegations. I'm sorry that no one could see this before and spare you the pain you are in. The question now is: Do you want to go live with her?"

Brandon tensed as his father was brought up, but he managed to nod. He finally found his voice and spoke. "Yes, sir, I would," he managed before his throat closed again.

"I think that it would be a great thing to see you stay with your grandmother. It's obvious that she loves you, and I believe that you will do nicely with her." The judge rose.

Is it really over? Was that all? Brandon though as he, too, rose and shook the judge's hand. The bailiff took him back to the waiting room.

Simeon guided the adult Brandon from the judge's chambers to the courtroom as the judge returned to the bench. He could see Lydia sitting at a table to the left side of the room. Behind her sat Peter Higgins. All testimony was over, and the attendees were preparing to hear the decision. Standing on the judge's right, Brandon saw, was the now-familiar image of God. He leaned over and spoke in the judge's ear. The judge finished looking through his paperwork and then looked at Lydia.

"I have seen and spoken with Brandon. I must say that his injuries are bad. Three broken ribs and a concussion are slow to heal. He is a very nervous young man, and I think I can understand why, but he was polite and well mannered. Mrs. Stevens, he would like to go home with you. He is in the waiting room now. I must caution that he is somewhat guarded, as can be expected. I only regret that we were unable to stop this before it happened. My ruling is that Robert Moore's parental rights be permanently revoked and custody be granted to Lydia Stevens. Good luck." With that, he pounded his gavel, rose, and left the room. Brandon could see God smiling and nodding.

"I can understand this now," Brandon said to Simeon. "I can see how God was working. He had His hand on me, even when I didn't know it."

"Yes, He did. Sometimes life doesn't work the way we want it to. Things happen that we can't explain, but God is in the midst of every situation. When bad things happen, God will use them for good. People just can't see it. Only He has the master plan, and trust is the important factor."

Lydia recalled the judge's words. Brandon had been like a frightened deer for so long; his eyes kept darting back and forth, as if looking for danger. She had immediately taken him from the courthouse to the nearest store. His clothes had been mere rags, showing the neglect from his father. A haircut had been needed, but it could wait. Clean clothes that fit properly could not. She hadn't gotten much that day because Brandon had been exhausted and physically hurting. She had gotten only the bare necessities, then she had taken him home and led him to his old room. She had kept everything the same. She knew that his tastes had changed, but until she knew what he liked now, the old sheets and things would have to do.

Brandon had walked into his room and looked around. Lydia had watched as some tension began to relax from his posture. He had gone to the bed and lain down, sitting up slightly when his grandmother brought him a soda and the painkillers his doctor had prescribed.

"Officer Higgins is coming to dinner tonight," Lydia had said quietly. "He said he had something to give back to you, but you have time for a long, well-deserved nap." With that, Lydia had left the room, closing the door behind her.

Brandon had slept for two solid hours. When he'd awakened, he walked slowly to the kitchen. Lydia had been at the stove, making Brandon's favorite dinner, spaghetti. Peter Higgins had sat at the table. Their conversation had stalled as Brandon had come into the room and eased into a chair. Before anyone could talk, Peter had reached into his pocket and withdrawn Brandon's pocket watch. Lydia's breath had caught when she saw it, and Brandon's eyes filled with tears.

"You asked me to keep it safe. Now it's time for you to have it back."

Without comment, Brandon had gently taken the watch and held it close. Finally, he had whispered, "Thank you."

CHAPTER 11

Simeon took Brandon back to his bedroom. Brandon needed a few moments to rest before they went further. Simeon knew that Brandon was coming around. He had seen God and he knew He was working in his life. Brandon had faced his past, and the healing process had begun.

Simeon slipped from Brandon's bedroom and into Lydia's. He smiled at the sight of her. God had allowed her to sleep for a short time, as hard memories can drive a person to exhaustion. He was glad she was resting. He would take this time to report on the progress and prepare for the rest of the night.

Unseen, Simeon crossed a threshold that took him out of the physical world and into the spiritual one. He was greeted by friends who gave encouraging words. They knew the importance of Simeon's task, and they knew that God had chosen well for this mission. Simeon would succeed.

He walked again into the Throne Room. God sat upon the ornate, royal chair with His Son on His right side. Both smiled as Simeon approached and bowed.

God spoke first. "You are doing well. Brandon's eyes are opening. It is good that he is resting, for there is much more for him to see tonight."

"Yes, Father. But the next phase will be harder. I do not know if I can witness that again." Simeon spoke with conviction.

This time, Christ's voice rose to greet him. "My friend, it is necessary. You and your colleagues comforted and strengthened me then, and now you must do the same for Brandon. It is the only way. He must see my gift, my Father's gift, to him." Christ's voice was full of the ever-present compassion that He was known for. Jesus knew how hard the rest of the night would be on His friend, but this assignment must be completed.

God spoke again, His voice clear and powerful. "Return to him. He is still resting, and he is remembering. Brandon is finally putting the pieces together and learning about my work with him. When it is time, I will send messengers to rouse the grandmother. For now, she has earned her sleep; however, the night continues for us all."

Simeon bowed again in deference to his Father and Lord and quickly departed. Brandon would need him soon.

Brandon lay on his bed as thoughts continued to race through his mind. He remembered the first morning he had awakened after returning to Lydia's care. He had opened his eyes and seen the familiar surroundings. It had all been exactly as it had been the day he had left. His posters were on the wall and toys lined his dresser. He had stopped playing with these things a long time ago; he had stopped playing at all. Between school and trying to keep the house clean for his dad, there had been no time for fun. He had gone from child to man in an instant.

The pain in his broken ribs was a constant reminder of what happened if he forgot one of his many chores. Although this beating was definitely the most severe, the beatings had occurred almost daily. Brandon had moved cautiously around Robert, fearing that his father would become angry.

That was over now, because Brandon was back with Lydia. Maybe he could learn how to be happy again; maybe he could learn to trust. He braced his side with his hand and sat up. He heard movement coming from the kitchen downstairs. Lydia was probably cooking breakfast. She had done that every morning for him when he had lived here with his mother. It had been a long time since anyone had cared for him like that. If he had wanted food at his dad's house, he had to fix it himself. He walked to the door and pulled it open. The welcoming scent of waffles hit his nose, and Brandon closed his eyes, sniffing appreciatively.

He went to the kitchen and sat at the table. He hadn't noticed last night, he had been too tired, but the room had been repainted. The bright yellow had been replaced with warm cream tones with blue trim. He liked it. Lydia set a plate in front of him, and he started eating ravenously.

"Brandon, we haven't prayed yet." Lydia's soft words weren't accusing, but they did hold a note of disappointment.

"What's the point? There is no God," Brandon tersely replied.

"You know that's not true. You asked Him into your life, remember?"

Brandon swallowed before answering. "I remember that you and Mom always talked about Him. I remember hearing that God would make her better, but He didn't. Now she's gone, and Dad hurt me. Like I said, there is no God."

Brandon finished his breakfast in silence. He took his plate to the sink, rinsed it off, and placed it in the dishwasher. He then walked back to the table and began clearing Lydia's dishes.

"Brandon, you don't have to do this. I'll clean up." Lydia was perplexed at both Brandon's words and his actions. He had never denied God before. She sent a quick prayer upward and decided to ignore his comments for now. He had endured a tough couple of years, and anger was a normal reaction. She would be patient and continue to pray for her grandson. God would show Brandon the truth in His own time, and in His own way, but they would be going to church in the next few days, and she needed to prepare Brandon for that.

Lydia rolled over on the bed. She was in that peaceful place somewhere between being asleep and being awake. Her mind wandered back to the first church service after Brandon's return.

He hadn't wanted to go. He hadn't yelled or thrown a tantrum; he had simply said that he wanted to stay home. Lydia had calmly explained that he had no alternative, he was going, so he had gotten out of bed and dressed.

He had been rather sullen when they had walked into the small cement building, but Lydia had overlooked him. She had so much to be thankful for on this day of worship, and she smiled as she greeted her friends inside. Many of them, she had known for her entire life. Her father had founded the church as an evangelist by starting a tent revival on the property more than fifty years earlier. The revival had lasted for so long that they had decided to buy the land and build a church, and it had flourished. Lydia's father had pastored it himself for nearly twenty years before retiring and passing the job to someone else. He had continued to do local services until the day he had passed away.

The church congregation had grown some since Brandon had been there last. They now had a youth pastor. It was a volunteer position, with zero benefits, but Tim Young did well. The teens related to him, and his lessons were filled with activities and deep discussions. Many times, Lydia had glanced in to find the small group huddled in earnest prayer, seeking the Lord. She had hoped that Tim and the teenagers he taught would reach out to Brandon so maybe he could find solace for his broken heart.

Brandon had dropped stubbornly into the pew. Although he hadn't been vocal in his rebellion, it had been clear from his posture that he would rather be anywhere but in church. The pastor had read the announcements and then welcomed Brandon personally from the pulpit. He had claimed that Brandon's presence was an answer to prayer. Brandon had blushed from the attention but remained silent. The congregation had then been released to go on to their various Sunday school classes.

Lydia had watched as a young girl and boy about Brandon's age approached them. She had listened as they asked him to join them in class. Brandon had started to refuse but then caught Lydia's eye. The boy had mentioned to Brandon that doughnuts and soda were served as snacks for the class, so Brandon had grudgingly followed them into a side room. Lydia had breathed a sigh of relief and sent a fleetingly prayer upward for her grandson.

Brandon remembered his caustic comments to the youth pastor and the class from his first Sunday at church with Lydia. They embarrassed him now, because he knew the teenagers had intended to be kind. They had sincerely wanted him to feel like he belonged with them, but the pain of his mother's death and father's abuse had made him feel different from the happy kids and their families. The publicity surrounding his father's arrest had put even more distance between Brandon and the others. Brandon knew that Lydia wouldn't reveal specific personal details, but he knew she would have asked for prayer for him. He had learned that she prayed a lot for his return, and he assumed that she would have prayed for his recovery as well. Because of this, he knew that the teens in the room, as well as their leader, would know about the injuries he had and how he had gotten them. The thought was unnerving. He had spent the entire hour lashing insults toward everyone in the room.

The youth pastor and the teens had continued to ask Brandon to join them for class, but after that initial class, Brandon would always refuse. He had wanted no part of the group or any of their activities. He had told Lydia that she could make him go but she couldn't make him participate. Lydia had eventually given up trying. He had gone along with her every time, without argument, but he would sit in the pew, sulking, the entire time.

This routine had continued all through Brandon's high school years. As Brandon's body had healed, so had his emotions. The forlorn, lonely boy had been replaced by a well-rounded, sociable young man. He had graduated at the top of his class with a full scholarship to a good college in California.

The sunny days in California were very enjoyable. He had made friends quickly and attended many parties. He had always put his schoolwork as his top priority, but he had plenty of time for a few beers with his friends. Church had become a memory, and so had Lydia's upbringing. He had been on his own and was making his own rules. That had all ended suddenly.

He had been at a social gathering and had partaken of too many beers. He could barely stand, and his girlfriend, Cassidy, had been no better. In Brandon's inebriated condition, his judgment was more than impaired. He had asked a friend who wasn't quite as drunk as he was to drive him to his dorm. Cassidy had decided to go with them. They had been rounding a curve, going way too fast, when his friend had lost control and slammed the car into a tree. Brandon had been thrown out the side window but, amazingly, hadn't been hurt. Neither had the driver. Cassidy, however, was a different story.

Brandon had sobered up quickly when he had realized that she was stuck, unconscious, in the car. The impact had driven the dash into her legs, and she was tightly pinned. About that time, his cell phone had rung, and he had absently answered. It was Lydia. He had told her what happened. She had managed to get enough information from him before hanging up on him to call for help. He was too dazed to even remember that she had called him. Help had arrived moments later. Cassidy had lived but was forever changed. Her right leg was amputated at the knee. She had never spoken to Brandon again. The driver of the car had been arrested and convicted of driving under the influence. Brandon had lost his scholarship for underage drinking. At least he hadn't been expelled. He had worked his way through school after that night, and he had never again touched an alcoholic drink.

Three lives had nearly been destroyed that night. All three of them had their demons to confront about that night. To Brandon, this was the worst memory yet. In every other experience, Brandon had been an innocent bystander, but he had been an active participant in this one.

Brandon sat up on the bed. Simeon hadn't returned yet. Brandon was feeling a little hungry, so he made his way to the kitchen. He would make himself a sandwich and wait.

CHAPTER 12

Brandon took his sandwich to the living room and sat down on the couch. He picked up the scrapbook of his articles that Lydia had been thumbing through earlier. As he ate his food, he absently flipped through the pages of the thick notebook.

Brandon felt Simeon enter the room rather than saw or heard him. "You're back."

"Yes." Simeon sat on the cushion beside Brandon and watched as he reread some of his articles. "You're very good at your job," he commented.

"Thank you. Most days, I enjoy writing. But sometimes a story really gets to me."

"God gave you your position, you know."

Brandon jolted a little. "I've seen where He has been in my past, but is He really that interested in the day-to-day aspects of life?"

"He is. You know that Mr. Evans believes. He has told you on numerous occasions that he has been praying for you. The day he received your application, he had been looking for a person to fill a specific need for his paper. He almost filed your application away for later, as his general policy is not to hire people straight out of school, but God told him to look again. He listened, and then when God said to hire you, he obeyed."

Brandon recalled a conversation with his boss that had similar qualities to the words he was hearing now. Mr. Evans did indeed prefer to hire applicants with more experience than Brandon had had at the time, but he had made an exception. Something in Brandon's portfolio had caught his eye. Mr. Evans had told him he had been looking for a person who could make an emotional appeal to his readers. He had said that he felt Brandon would fulfill the role nicely.

Simeon approached another topic. "Tell me about your first assignment with the *Journal*."

Brandon sighed. These were also deep memories. "A house fire ripped a family apart. A mother and father were sleeping in bed. Two boys slept in another bedroom, while the youngest child, a girl, shared the room with her parents. The family had been unable to move to a larger home, due to financial complications. The fire killed the father and the two older children. In an instant, a family of five became a family of two."

Brandon lifted the piece of newspaper from the pages of his scrapbook. His thoughts drifted back to that night. He could still smell the smoke lingering in the cool air just before dawn. The mother, a young woman looking barely old enough to have a family, had clung to her toddler, the only child to survive. A kind neighbor had wrapped a thin blanket around them, and the woman had held it tightly as she watched her life burn. Brandon had lifted his camera and snapped a picture, and the *Journal* had included it with the article. One could easily see the fragility of life in the simple snapshot.

"The family was living paycheck to paycheck. The furnace wasn't working properly, and they didn't know. It was located in the back of the house, right under the children's bedroom. The furnace blew and took the back side of the house completely off. The brothers were killed instantly. The explosion woke the parents. The mother grabbed the toddler and ran from the house, while the father tried in vain to get to the others. The second explosion took his life."

Brandon had tried for months to get the images of raw grief out of his head. He had yet to succeed. The mother and child had picked up the shattered pieces if their lives and moved on. A successful lawsuit against a negligent landlord had provided financial security, but they had never fully recovered. The article Brandon had written had begun a wave of pieces on tenant-landlord situations as well as safety issues to prevent more tragedies. He hoped that something good had come of his work for someone, but the tragedy for the family had been great. He wished he could write about positive stories instead of the continuous emotional pieces he was assigned to.

"How does God do it?" Brandon asked, his voice barely above a whisper. "How does He sit back and watch as humanity suffers and destroys itself? This woman and her child suffered terribly. My father destroyed my life. Every day, children are kidnapped, innocent people are murdered, and some languish through pain that would be worse than death."

"You've seen how God weeps with His children. He agonizes along with those He loves."

Brandon took a few moments to digest Simeon's words. He couldn't help but ask himself why. Finally, Brandon put his voice to the words that rang in his head. "How did man fall so far from God?"

Simeon stood and held out his arm. "Let me show you."

The familiar sensation of the room spinning as time changed assaulted Brandon. When his feet became steady again, he noticed a vast garden. Everywhere he looked, he saw trees and various plants. There were giant redwoods, maples, and oaks. Apple, pear, and orange trees bent with the weight of their succulent fruit. The larger trees allowed grape vines to twist and turn up the trunks, and large clusters of juicy grapes, both white and red, brought a splash of color to the rough brown bark.

Brandon heard a noise behind him, and he turned to see a giant gorilla rambling toward him. Instinctively, he stepped back, only to fall backward. He landed next to a mother ape that was busy nursing her baby. He rolled away and got back on his feet. He was certain that the animals would be angry at his intrusion, but to his surprise, they showed no fear or signs of aggression. The baby gorilla turned to look at Brandon. Slowly, he left his mother and lumbered over to Brandon. The animal reached out and stroked Brandon's leg. Brandon bent over and let the young ape explore his face with his weathered hands.

He looked up at Simeon. "Where are we?"

"This is Eden. We are at the beginning of time on earth. God regularly communed with His creation, as there was nothing to separate them. Listen. Man walks here, for now."

Brandon couldn't see anyone, but he could hear the footsteps of someone passing through the trees. He strained to see but failed in his attempt. The greenery was too lush and dense to see through.

Suddenly, a voice boomed through the peaceful setting. "Where are you?" the question resonated. Brandon listened for an answer, but all he could hear was the sound of sobbing echoing through the trees.

"Man has fallen. This is the beginning of sin and death. Everything that happens from now is a result of what took place in this garden. This is where God and Man were separated and God began His plan for reconciliation."

Instantly, the land became cracked and barren. Brandon could see a man and woman huddled together as they made their way up the steep, rocky mountain. The wind picked up its pace, and Brandon shivered from the cold. He glanced across his shoulder, searching for the peaceful shelter of the garden. Instead, his eyes met those of a towering angel holding a flaming sword in his hand.

"There is no return, and nothing is provided now. It must be earned with hard work and perseverance. Everything has a price, including the pride and rebellion that brought us here. Backs will bend and hearts will break as man fights for his survival, but it will be achieved, and life will continue. Every person has his own Eden experience. Although the world isn't perfect, there will come a time for everyone when a decision must be made. For you, Brandon, that time will be tonight. There is much left for you to see first."

CHAPTER **13**

Day turned to night, and the stars shone brightly. The moon was full, and Brandon was perched on the top of a hill, looking over a small town. The homes and other structures were made of dirt and brick, and even at this hour, the town seemed bustling with activity. Candles and lamps cast a soothing glow from the many dwellings. People rushed around the streets and congregated to discuss the day's events.

Brandon's eyes focused on a man leading a small donkey while a woman, wrapped tightly in her robes, clung to the animal's back, trying desperately to keep her balance. The man walked to the nearest building and knocked at the door. The occupant opened the door, only to slam it closed again right away. The man stood on the stoop for a moment before turning back to the woman. He walked back to her, to the donkey's reins, and went to the next building. The results were the same.

The couple coursed down the street, rapping on every door they passed. One by one, each possibility declined to offer aid. Brandon could see the woman was in pain. She was sweating profusely and breathing rapidly. Her hand continually moved to her abdomen as if she were cradling it. Brandon glanced questioningly at Simeon.

"God's plan, formed in Eden, began to unfold here, on this night." Simeon looked back to the couple. "Mary and Joseph have traveled a long way. They are seeking shelter, but the city has many visitors, and there is none to be found."

The couple reached the last building on the busy street. They were close enough now for Brandon to hear their conversation. He realized that the language barrier had been removed, and amazingly, he could understand every word. Joseph was explaining to Mary that this inn was their last hope for a place to stay. He raised his hand and knocked. An innkeeper opened the door and started to refuse, when a soft moan broke through the lips of the woman. The host looked at her, and compassion filled his face. He turned back to his visitor. "I have no room for you here. I cannot give you shelter at my inn. But up the hill, in a small cave, is where I keep my animals. You may stay there."

Joseph gave the innkeeper a grateful smile and turned the donkey toward the opening in the hillside. Slowly, he made his way up the incline, leading his mount up the worn, rocky path. Together, they disappeared into the cave.

The landscape changed, and Brandon found himself in a grassy valley. The lowing of sheep on the surrounding hills caught his attention. He looked down and noticed that his jeans and t-shirt were gone, and in their place was the garb of a poverty-stricken man from earlier times. He could smell the acidic stench of sweat mixed with animal odors. His nose wrinkled in distaste.

From his left, he heard Simeon whisper in his ear, "Experience this night for yourself." Brandon turned to find his friend, but Simeon was gone. He slowly pivoted as he took in his surroundings.

The sheep were not the only ones on the knolls. Scattered throughout the large flock were several men and boys of various ages. Like Brandon, he wore clothing that was tattered and filthy. One man caught Brandon's eye and smiled, revealing rotten and missing teeth. The man seemed friendly enough, so Brandon made his way toward him.

"Evening, young man. Are you new here? I haven't seen you before."

"Yes, sir. I'm afraid that I don't know anyone."

"Never mind about that. You will get to know them soon enough. There's a different feel in the air tonight, and we don't quite know what to think of it. Even the sheep feel it. They are a little agitated tonight. Never have seen the likes of it."

Brandon watched the sheep for a moment. He had never been around the animals before, but he quickly noticed what the old shepherd had. The sheep mulled around with their heads together, almost like they were talking to each other. At times they would look to the sky as if expecting something. Brandon found himself looking toward the stars as well.

Behind him came a noise, and he whirled around. The sky was lit up brightly. It almost looked to be daylight, except for the dark lines surrounding the resplendent sight. The shepherds of the field were gathering around him now. Many were frozen in fear as others knelt in terrified respect. Something powerful was here.

A familiar-looking man stood in the light, and for a moment, Brandon thought it was Simeon. He looked closer and realized that it was not his friend but another angel. The angel spoke, his voice loud and clear. "Do not be afraid, for I have good news. Tonight is born a baby, and He will be your Savior. Go to Him. He is in a manger, in Bethlehem. He will be wrapped in strips of cloth."

As the angel finished speaking, the sky became filled with angels. Both Lydia and Rachel had read Brandon this story many times in his youth, but now he was seeing these majestic events unfold in front of him. Tears pooled in his eyes and spilled down his cheeks. What a gift he was being given.

The angels burst into joyous song. "Glory to God in the highest heaven, and on earth, peace to those who have His goodwill!"

As they sang, the light shifted to illuminate a path leading to the cave that housed the infant. The shepherds humbly but excitedly began to walk down toward it. Brandon followed as the glorious music lingered in his ears.

It didn't take long for the group to reach their destination. Brandon remained outside for a moment, nerves keeping him from entering. He could hear the bleating of the animals that called this primitive stable home. The wind carried the smell of dung and straw through the hillside and down into the valley. As he waited, gathering his courage, he saw a small boy walking toward him.

The child was wearing the clothing Brandon related to the shepherds, a tunic and a robe for warmth. He was young, maybe only ten or so, and he walked with a pronounced limp. Brandon crossed over to him and helped him finish his climb.

"Thank you, sir," the boy said. "I heard the singing and saw the angels. I wanted to come too, but I'm slower than everyone else."

"What's your name?" Brandon asked the child.

"Samuel." Brandon smiled at the whistling noise that came with the *S*. Samuel had lost his front teeth, and they had yet to grow back in.

"Well, Samuel, are you ready to go in?"

Samuel's smile crashed. "I don't know. I'm a little scared."

Brandon held out his hand. "You know what, Samuel? I am too. Why don't we go in together and see what all the fuss is about?"

Samuel's grin was instantaneous. The two clasped hands and went into the stable. The light was very dim, as there was only a small lantern lit in the back. An opening in the top of the cave provided the only way for air to circulate, so it was smothering in the tiny room, especially because the shepherds were now crowded in the tiny space. Donkeys and oxen were tethered to makeshift stalls along the wall, their evening meal of hay scattered in front of them. The animals seemed to be watching the proceedings with curiosity.

On the far side of the enclosure lay a woman, resting with an infant in her arms. The man was nervous as he tried to make the new mother comfortable. He looked toward the shepherds and grimaced, shooing them back outside. "I'm sorry," he began, "but she is very tired. As you can see, she just had a baby and needs her rest. Please come back later."

Disappointed, the men started to turn and leave, but then the woman's timid voice stopped them. "Wait," she said before turning to her companion. "Joseph, this baby is not for us alone. Please, let them come and see. We cannot keep this gift from them, for He was sent for them too."

Her words seemed to soothe the agitated man, and he acquiesced to her pleadings. "You are right, Mary. We are meant to share Him, for He is not ours alone."

The filthy men lowered themselves to the floor. There they sat in stunned silence as they gazed upon the child. Soon, many of the men were openly crying, and even more were fighting tears as they tried to break loose.

After a few moments, Mary seemed to notice Brandon and Samuel standing in the back of the room. The boy was trembling in his effort not to cry.

"Child, some here," came the sweet voice of the new mother. Samuel looked to Brandon for confirmation, and Brandon nodded his encouragement. Slowly, Samuel released Brandon's hand and limped toward the family. He cautiously glanced at Joseph and visibly relaxed as the man smiled at him. The boy reached the baby and knelt down beside Him.

Samuel gazed into the bright eyes of the newborn. The dark curls were still damp from birth. "May I touch him?" the child softly asked the mother. "I've never seen a baby before. I'm the youngest of all my brothers and sisters."

Mary nodded, and the boy gently stroked the baby's pink cheek. Mary looked thoughtful for a moment, almost as if she were listening to something. Then she spoke. "Would you like to hold him?"

Samuel looked shocked, scared, and excited all at once. "I can? I won't break Him?"

Mary chuckled. "No, He will be fine." She looked toward Joseph. "Will you help him?"

Joseph nodded and took the baby from His mother. Samuel sat down and waited. The child was placed in his arms as Joseph helped him cradle the baby's head correctly. Everyone in the room fell silent as Samuel began to sing to the infant. Throughout the song, he rocked the baby, until soon, the newborn was peacefully sleeping. Samuel looked up at Mary and Joseph. Silent tears were streaming down Samuel's face. "My mother used to sing to me. I haven't seen her in a long time. I got hurt and my family didn't have a lot of money, so we couldn't afford a doctor. That's why I can't walk right. I know they love me. I have to work with the sheep to help get food. All of my brothers are shepherds too, so as soon as I got old enough, I went to live with the flocks. I haven't been home since. I miss them."

The baby began to stir, and Joseph handed him back to Mary to nurse. The shepherds took the cue and quietly began to leave. Brandon waited for Samuel, who wanted to give the baby one last kiss, then the two of them walked out as well.

They were halfway down the slope when Brandon realized something. "Samuel, you're…"

"I know. My leg is fixed. I walk fine now." The boy was openly crying. Brandon stopped moving, too overcome to continue. He sat down on the dirt and wept. In the distance, he heard someone call to Samuel, and with a quick good-bye, the boy ran off to join the shepherds. Brandon sat, alone, trying to process what he had experienced. He had felt the raw power in that cramped stable, he had heard the tenderness from Mary, and he had seen the lives changed. Only one word could describe the night: awesome.

CHAPTER **14**

Simeon returned and found Brandon still sitting on the ground. Although dazed, Brandon had regained his composure. "I can't begin to describe it. Amazing, awesome, exhilarating; nothing seems adequate. I've built a career around words, and I am unable to find one that encompasses everything that I have seen and felt here tonight."

Simeon reflected on his own memories. "It was the same for us, but from a different perspective. God's plan was unfolding, and the human race would have a way back to Him. That little baby came straight from Heaven. We missed Him, we worried over Him, we wept for Him. Man had their Savior, but we were missing our King. It was a bittersweet moment."

As Simeon spoke, the surroundings changed again, transforming from a dirt path to a green bluff. The grass felt soft under Brandon, and he was tempted to lie down. The thought passed as he heard voices coming up behind him, and he glanced over his shoulder to see who was coming. There were many people talking amongst themselves. Several times, fingers pointed in the direction of one man.

He looked familiar to Brandon, and after a few seconds, Brandon recognized Him. "It's Jesus!" he exclaimed, and Simeon nodded in confirmation.

"He is no longer a baby. He is now a grown man, and He is building a reputation for being a most unusual teacher. Instead of tradition and judgment, He talks of love and forgiveness. It is a message that people have longed to hear."

Jesus sat on a rock protruding from the incline, and He began to speak. Gentleness and compassion were the impressions that crossed Brandon's mind when he heard His soft voice. Brandon looked through the crowd. Everywhere, people were mesmerized by His words.

"Blessed are those who recognize they are spiritually helpless. The Kingdom of Heaven belongs to them. Blessed are those who mourn. They will be comforted."

Brandon was startled at those words. He snapped his eyes toward Jesus and saw that He was staring straight back at Brandon. It was as if Jesus was speaking directly to Brandon. He thought about his time of mourning. He had never been comforted.

Simeon spoke, as if reading Brandon's mind. "He offered His comfort, but His attempt was denied.

You wouldn't allow yourself to be comforted. He can give only what is accepted."

Simeon's words struck Brandon's heart. Simeon was right. Brandon had shut everyone out in his grief. He had hardened his heart and refused to let anyone close. The result had been loneliness and bitterness.

Jesus was still teaching. "Blessed are those who are gentle. They will inherit the earth. Blessed are those who hunger and thirst for God's approval. They will be satisfied."

Brandon thought about Lydia and Rachel. Both of them could be described as gentle, and they certainly sought after God's heart. They prayed, and not just with their words. They meant what they said, and then they listened for His response. Rachel was now with God, and that was definitely achieving God's approval. Brandon listened through the rest of Jesus' teaching, but his mind was racing. After a while, Jesus stopped talking and got up to leave.

Simeon rose to his feet and helped Brandon to his. "We cannot follow, as we only have a short time and there is much to cover. Let us move ahead a little."

Brandon could smell the salt water before he could see it. A boat was floating on the sea as it moved toward the shore. The atmosphere was tense, but he couldn't find a reason for it. The boat reached the shore, and Brandon saw that several men, including Jesus were on board. People milled around on the shore, waiting for Christ to step off the boat and speak to them.

As soon as Jesus' feet touched the sand grazing the water, an ear-piercing scream broke through, slicing the air. Everyone stared as a man ran toward the crowd, aiming for Christ. His hair hung in wild tangles around his face. He had no clothes on, and broken chains hung loosely around his wrists and ankles. His body bore the scars of repeated injury. He reminded Brandon of the subject of a story he had once written about self-mutilation.

As the man neared, women grabbed their children in fear, but the crazed man was focused on only one person: Jesus. He stopped when he reached Him, falling at His feet. "Why are you bothering me, Jesus, Son of the Most High God?" were his excruciating cries. "Why are You torturing me?"

Jesus focused on the man, His gaze seeming to pierce the man's soul. He paused briefly before speaking, asking for the man's name. The man's bellows intensified, becoming unearthly and positively inhuman.

"My name is Legion!" This man was clearly possessed and was host to numerous evil spirits. "Please, Master, do not send us to the Pit! Instead, let us go to the pigs grazing nearby!" As one, the demons begged Jesus not to force them to their doom.

Jesus granted their request, and the transition was immediate. Brandon watched in horror as the pigs jolted from the sudden impact. The terrorized animals ran wildly, finally reaching the sea, where they all drowned. The crowd, once anticipating the arrival and teachings of Christ, were now begging in fear for Him to leave. They begged Him to leave. He returned to the boat but turned as someone tugged on his sleeve. The calm man standing there bore little resemblance to the crazed lunatic from earlier. Someone had been thoughtful enough to give him a robe to cover his naked body. He bowed and begged, "Please, Lord, take me with You."

Jesus smiled. "No. You need to stay here. Go back to your family, and tell them what has happened. Show them what God has done for you." With that, Jesus stepped back into the boat and was pushed away from the shore.

Simeon turned to Brandon. "Jesus will not stay when He is asked to leave. Some are meant to travel with Him, and others are meant to do His work in different ways. This man was to be a witness in his own town and with his own family. Everyone has his own position to fill. But demonic entities are not the only things submissive to Christ."

Brandon and Simeon were now in the middle another throng. There was absolutely no way to move, as people pressed in on all sides. Brandon felt an elbow to his back as he was shoved forward into the person in front of him, and then he was immediately shoved to the side, caught in another wave of motion. He would have fallen had there been room. Simeon was feeling similar movements around him. Everyone was being jostled back and forth.

"What's going on?" Brandon had to yell for Simeon to hear him, even though they were right next to each other.

"Jesus is walking by this way. He has become extremely popular with His unusual style of ministry and astonishing miracles. Some say that the devil is in Him. Others believe that He is the Son of God. The sick and tormented from everywhere flock to Him, hoping for a blessing. Look, even now, one comes."

Brandon strained to see the person making his or her way to Christ. It was impossible to see through the massive sea of bodies. As he searched, he felt something graze his ankle. Reaching down to brush it away, he was startled when he touched another hand. He looked down and saw the covered head of a small woman. Her gnarled hands spoke of age, illness, and hard work. Brandon noticed her quivering shoulders and knew she was crying as she struggled against the flow of the crowd. He could barely hear the words she spoke as she tried valiantly to push forward. "Jesus. I will get to Him. Just His clothes. I only need to touch His clothes," she chanted, and Brandon winced as a foot connected with her head.

"She's going to get trampled! No one sees her!"

"Patience. She has perseverance, and she has faith. God honors both."

Brandon watched as the woman painfully, yet determinedly, kept crawling through the crowd. His eyes followed her until she had been consumed completely by the throng of people. He kept searching for her, hoping she was all right. After what seemed like an eternity, the people stopped moving as a voice cut through the ensuing silence.

"Who touched me?" The words help no malice, no contempt.

The people parted, leaving the woman standing alone. Fearfully, she made her way to Christ and knelt. "I did, my Lord. Please don't be angry. I only wanted to be healed, for my body has been broken for so long."

Jesus lowered Himself until he faced the sobbing woman. Cupping her chin and lifting her face, He smiled softly. "Daughter. Do not be afraid. Your faith has made you well."

The woman clung to Him, her tears changing to those of gratefulness. "Thank You, Lord," she kept repeating.

Brandon watched the scene, astonished at what was before him. Simeon offered a brief explanation. "She has been bleeding for twelve years. Every cent has gone to doctors and their cures. In this culture, blood makes a person dirty. Any person coming in contact with her also becomes unclean, so she lives in isolation. But now, her life can begin again."

It was hard to deny Jesus' effect on the people. There was no refuting the power He had over sickness and disease. Brandon's attention stopped on a group of men standing on the periphery of the crowd. They were whispering to each other while their eyes shot daggers at Jesus.

"Some men are jealous of the attention my King receives. He teaches of a loving Father instead of a god who is angry and unattainable. These lessons usurp the authority these religious men have. Trouble is brewing, and Jesus is at the center of the drama."

The seaside faded as a mountain came into view. Rough holes had been hewn into the face of the rocky slope. The area looked abandoned and despairing.

"This is an area of graves. To come here and touch death is defilement for the people in the area. God's law forbids it. There are many laws existing at this time. It was a consequence of sin. Because there is separation from God, a pious life is required to achieve righteousness. This is why God sent His Son. Man needed a way to access God again."

Brandon heard loud laments and keening coming up the mountain. A group of mourners were approaching, and Jesus was in the center of them.

"Jesus' friend Lazarus is buried here. He has been dead for four days. His sisters walk beside Jesus. They wanted Him to come earlier, hoping for their brother to be healed, but Jesus waited. By the time He ventured toward the city of Bethany, where Lazarus and his sisters lived, Lazarus was already dead. Now Jesus wants to see the grave."

The group of people stopped in front of the tomb's entrance. Brandon was moved to see Jesus weeping.

"I've told you that Christ grieves when we grieve. Lazarus was a close friend," Simeon responded to the unspoken question.

Jesus stopped crying and took a deep breath. He was aware of the murmurs against Him. Brandon could hear them as well. Some were saying that Jesus had healed before, some were asking why He hadn't hurried to Lazarus's side when He heard of the illness instead of tarrying and letting Lazarus die.

Jesus straightened His back and turned toward some of the men in the group. "Remove the stone," He commanded. The people were surprised at this. One of the sisters tugged at His arm.

"Master, my brother has been dead for four days. By now, his body stinks."

Jesus turned to her. "Martha, didn't I tell you that if you believe, you will see God's glory?" Martha stared at Jesus for a moment and then directed the men to do as He said, and the stone was pulled away. Brandon heard Jesus pray.

"Father, I thank You for hearing me. You always hear me, but I want the crowd to believe that You sent me." With those words, He looked straight into the tomb and yelled, "Lazarus! Come out!" Brandon fell backward when a body, completely covered in cloth, emerged from the grave. He wasn't the only one reacting. Many people screamed, fearing that they were seeing a ghost. The body struggled against the wrappings that held him tight, so Jesus told the men to free the man from them. The grave clothes were removed, and Lazarus's sisters ran joyously to their brother. The excited crowd departed, leaving Brandon and Simeon alone once again.

"Jesus did many things in the three years of His ministry. I did not have time to show you everything, so I chose these three events because I wanted you to see the power and authority that Christ had. He can order demons, He can heal diseases, and He can reverse death. One would think that He would have been greatly received amongst His people."

"Wasn't He?" Brandon asked.

Simeon's voice held a trace of sadness that left Brandon confused and concerned. "Both yes and no. The religious leaders were jealous as they lost control of the people. They didn't like it, and they sought a way to stop Jesus. They eventually found a weakness, and they used it."

CHAPTER **15**

Once again, Brandon found himself wearing a tunic indicative of the time. He was sitting near a long, low table, where men reclined as they were eating. Brandon saw Lazarus as well as others he recognized as Jesus' disciples. Martha was serving the food, and Mary was nowhere to be seen.

"Here she comes," Simeon said softly. He was sitting next to Brandon, similarly dressed.

"Who?" Brandon whispered back.

"Mary."

A young woman entered the room, her eyes nervously darting back and forth. She was clutching something in her hands, and she stopped for a moment to survey the room. She laid her hand on her stomach, as if willing it to settle, and then continued through the room until she reached Jesus. Slowly, she knelt in front of him and revealed the small bottle she had been carrying. She opened it, and a sweet, yet spicy, fragrance filled the air. With tears streaming down her face, she poured the oil over Jesus' feet and began rubbing them.

Brandon could see mixed reactions on everyone's face. One man leaned over to Jesus and vocally criticized the actions. Simeon leaned over and spoke in Brandon's ear. "This is Judas Iscariot. He is the treasurer of the group. He is rebuking Mary, saying that the perfume is being wasted, it should have been sold and the money given to the poor, yet his words do not match his heart. He is greedy."

Jesus spoke to Judas. "Leave her alone. She is preparing my body to be buried. The poor will always be with you, but my time is growing short."

Judas looked startled, as if he had been slapped, his face flushing in embarrassment and anger. Mary removed her head covering and revealed long dark tresses. She used her hair to dry Jesus' feet as the rest of the men and women in the room watched.

Brandon glanced back at Judas. He could see the seething hatred on the man's face. "He is dangerous," he commented as much to himself as to Simeon.

"Yes, he is, but not tonight." Simeon smiled. "Tomorrow we will celebrate."

With that, the room became city streets lined with people. Simeon and Brandon were still dressed to fit in with the revelers. Simeon wore a look of pure joy that Brandon had never seen on his face. Everyone was happy and laughing, and Brandon saw that many of them were carrying palm branches in their hands. People were shouting, "Hosanna! Blessed is the one who comes in the name of the Lord, the King of Israel!"

"They are praising my King!" Simeon laughingly told Brandon. "It is always delightful to hear!"

Brandon looked and saw a small donkey carrying Jesus on its back. Jesus' disciples followed, caught up in the moment. They were waving and hugging each other as they walked behind their leader down the city streets. Only Judas looked discontented and uncomfortable. Brandon observed as he met the eyes of the religious leaders that were paying close attention as things were unfolding. He caught the nearly imperceptible nod that Judas sent their way. Something was going on. Brandon's instincts were screaming, and he didn't know why. Trouble was certainly coming.

Brandon found himself on the abandoned street later that night. The evidence of the partying was scattered across the walkways and around the buildings. Gone were the worshippers; they were now inside for the night. Brandon was once again in his jeans and t-shirt. He picked up a nearby frond from a palm tree. He played with it a moment as his thoughts returned to the singing and dancing he had just witnessed. Christ deserved the honors, he knew that, but he couldn't shake the sense of the foreboding that had overtaken him.

Simeon placed his hand on Brandon's arm. Silently, he guided them to a small room on the upper floor of a nearby building. The building itself was made of stone. It was a simple structure with windows cut into the rock. An outdoor stairwell led up, and the two of them ascended these steps. Still not speaking, they entered the room, unseen by the occupants.

Jesus and his disciples were reclining around a table, eating their evening meal. Jesus seemed distracted. He stood and walked to the side of the room, where He retrieved a towel and a basin of water. He then walked back and began to wash and dry his friends' feet. One, Brandon heard him called Peter, began to argue with Jesus but then quickly relented. Once Jesus had completed His task, He told the men that they must do as He had just done. The meaning was clear: If you want to lead, you must learn to follow. Jesus' next words broke Brandon's heart. "One of you will betray me." The words were soft, belying the strong implications. The men began to talk amongst themselves. Finally, one got the courage to ask who the treasonous man was.

Jesus took a piece of bread and dipped it into the wine. He then stood and said, "It is the one that I give this bread to." He angled toward Judas and handed him the morsel. "Please. Go quickly and do what you must."

Judas ran from the room, leaving a shocked silence in his wake.

"The night is still young, and terrible events will happen. Everyone is leaving. Jesus wants to pray. His strength is dwindling," Simeon said with a deep sadness. Just as Brandon had never heard the joy in Simeon's voice before the earlier worship, he had never before heard this despair in his friend's voice.

They followed the men to a nearby garden, where olive trees grew rampant. Jesus turned to His friends, speaking with great sadness. "All of you will abandon me tonight. Scripture says, 'I will strike the shepherd, and the sheep in the flock will be scattered.' But after I am brought back to life, I will go to Galilee ahead of you."

His friends began murmuring their protests between each other. Peter was vehement. "Even if everyone else abandons you," he replied, "I never will."

Jesus shook His head and told Peter that he would deny Him three times before morning. The rash disciple didn't believe Jesus and continued to protest. Jesus turned away, needing to be alone. The disciples found places to sit as Jesus continued ahead. "Pray," was the only request He made. Brandon watched as the tired men attempted to pray but soon fell asleep.

He looked through the trees and saw Jesus kneeling in prayer. Jesus was quaking with the burden of His words. "Father, please, take this cup from me. However, Your will must be done, not mine." Jesus was openly weeping. Brandon could see the exhaustion settling in. Then, behind Jesus, an angel descended, carried on a wave of light. The heavenly presence seemed to renew Jesus' strength, and in time, Jesus stood. Brandon looked closer. Flecks of red were on the ground. Concerned, he glanced at Jesus. He was wiping sweat from his forehead, and there was blood mixed in with it.

"Is He actually sweating blood?"

"Yes. He is greatly distressed. He will suffer much during the night and following day. It is His gift to man; to you."

Jesus had no sooner returned to his friends and roused them than loud footsteps were heard in the leaves. Brandon could see Roman soldiers approaching Jesus. "No," he whispered.

"Not again," Simeon begged.

Before Brandon could comment, Peter whipped out a sword. In one swift movement, he cut off the ear of a young boy. The night air was filled with painful screams. Jesus looked at the rash disciple and picked the ear off the ground. Quickly, he healed the injury and went willingly with the soldiers.

"It has started," Simeon woefully said. "It cannot be stopped. The sacrifice will be lovingly made for mankind."

Brandon saw the disciples run away and hide in fear. Several followed at a distance, curious about the fate of their teacher. Brandon and Simeon followed the soldiers, as they could not be seen. They found themselves in front of the Jewish council.

Jesus stood in the center of the mob. All around Him were the religious leaders in Jerusalem. Brandon listened as, one by one, witnesses were led in. Testimony was presented that, even to Brandon's untrained ear, was obviously false. The chief priest, Caiaphas, repetitively asked Christ for His response to the declarations, yet Jesus remained silent. Then He was pointedly asked if He was the Son of God. His response was, "Yes, I am. I guarantee that from now on, you will see the Son of Man in the highest position in Heaven. He will be coming on the clouds of Heaven." This statement further enraged the council.

The chief priest was so angered that he ripped his clothes. He yelled and accused Jesus of blasphemy. The verdict was guilty, and the council wanted execution. Because they could not carry this out, they settled for a sound beating, at least for the moment. When it was over, Jesus was sent to Pontius Pilate for final sentencing.

Brandon's thoughts returned to the disciples. He turned questioningly to Simeon. "Do His followers know where He is, what is happening to Him?"

Simeon looked discouraged. "They do. They are watching from a distance. Peter has denied knowledge of Christ. He was scared, and that fear led to self-preservation. Right now, anyone connected with Jesus is in danger of arrest and possible execution."

"What of Judas? What was his reward for his treachery?"

Simeon took them to a barren field. In the distance, Brandon could see an old tree, void of any signs of life. Leaves did not grace the broken and gnarled limbs. From the thickest branch, a body, hung by a rope tied around its neck.

"The religious leaders paid him well. He received thirty pieces of silver for handing Jesus over to them. When he came to his senses and realized that his act had condemned Christ, he felt regret. He tried to take his betrayal back, but to no avail. He used the money to buy this field, and then he committed suicide. I'm assuming he thought he couldn't ask for forgiveness. After all, his actions had just killed God."

Brandon let the words sink in. "What happens next for Him?" Brandon dreaded the answer as much as he anticipated it.

"He is going to the governor's mansion. There, Pilate will continue the trial."

The mansion appeared in all of its glory. Marble columns supported stone terraces with intricate carvings and details. Pilate himself sat on an ornate throne. His robes were deep purple, indicating his royal status, and he wore a crown of delicate golden leaves. He watched as leaders from the Jewish nation brought their prisoner forward.

Brandon's breath caught at the sight of Jesus. A lump formed in his throat as he took in the bruised and marred face. Jesus was unrecognizable, as both His eyes were black and blood had dried and caked on his swollen and cracked lips.

"Why have you brought me this man?" Pilate commanded.

The leaders all spoke at once, with all of their accusations. Pilate held up his hand, and silence ensued. Finally, Caiaphas spoke. "We found that He stirs up trouble among the people. He keeps them from paying their taxes to the emperor, and He says that He is Christ, a king!"

Pilate stood and looked down at the battered man. "Are you the king of the Jews?"

"Yes, I am," was Jesus' quiet, but firm, response.

Pilate was thoughtful for a moment, and then he surprised everyone by saying, "I can't find this man guilty of any crime."

The comment caused such a reaction that Pilate had to gesture again for silence. Another leader yelled out that Jesus had stirred up people throughout Judea, including Galilee. Upon hearing that, Pilate asked if Jesus was from Galilee. When he received confirmation, he ordered Jesus to be taken to King Herod, who happened to be visiting Jerusalem at that time.

Jesus was taken to yet another person for sentencing. Word of His reputation had reached the king, and Herod wanted to see Him. Brandon winced as Herod was sarcastic and rude to Jesus. Herod wanted Christ to perform a miracle for him, but Jesus wouldn't give in to Herod's cajoling. Jesus was asked several questions, and as was His nature, He didn't answer any of them, so Herod and his soldiers used Christ as amusement for a while before putting a colorful robe on His shoulders as an ironic response to

Jesus' claim of royalty and returning Him to Pilate. Herod's verdict was not guilty.

Brandon couldn't understand what he was seeing. He asked his questions to Simeon. "If Jesus was found innocent not once, but twice, then why are they continuing this farce?"

"This was God's plan. From the beginning of time, sin had to be paid for with innocent blood. The usual sacrifice was a lamb without faults, a perfect specimen. This atonement came with rigid rules and regulations. God didn't want to be known as a stranger, a cold and heartless ruler. He wanted His people to know how compassionate and loving He actually is. He sent His perfect Lamb to erase every sin that man had committed and will continue to commit. Jesus came willingly. This is an offering from both the Father and the Son."

CHAPTER 16

B randon found Jesus once more in the courtyard of the governor's mansion as His trial continued. Pilate received Him from Herod with a feeling of anxiety. He could not condemn an innocent man to death. Pilate turned from the crowd as his wife, Claudia, stepped up to him. "Please, Pontius, may I have a word before you proceed?"

Pilate and his wife left the room for a private conference.

"What do you need, my dear?"

Claudia hesitated. "I had a most disturbing dream last night. It has bothered me all day. This man that stands before you is innocent. We cannot shed his blood in death. I fear the gods will torment us if we do."

"Claudia, listen to the crowd. It is riotous! What am I supposed to do? The people cry for His death."

"Have Him whipped. Maybe a public flogging will satisfy them. If not, follow your tradition of offering one prisoner's freedom. Find the most violent man in prison and offer a choice, him or this Jesus. Certainly, sense will take hold of these people and they will make the right choice."

Pilate listened to his wife. Her logic seemed sound. With a long look in her husband's direction, Claudia took her leave and Pilate returned to his courtyard to pronounce sentencing.

Upon his entrance, silence fell among the onlookers. Pilate stood and reflected on the proceedings, still struggling to find some understanding of what was taking place before him. Finding his voice, he announced, "I find no fault with this man. Herod has also found Him innocent; however, to quench your thirst for blood, I will have Him whipped."

Pilate turned toward his soldiers and nodded. The men took Jesus to carry out the order. The soldiers stripped Jesus of the robes placed on Him by Herod and pushed him toward a wooden pole. Iron cuffs hung down the sides of the post. It was evident that intended victims would have no way to escape this punishment. Brandon shuttered as he saw dark brown blood stains spattered around the area.

One of the soldiers roughly placed Jesus' wrists inside the primitive shackles. Another moved to a nearby table and picked up a mean-looking whip. Brandon had assumed that the instrument of torture would have resembled a horse whip, but he was sorely mistaken. This had several leather straps secured together by a thick band. On each strap, shards of glass were adhered to the rough material. This device was obviously meant to inflict severe pain and bring about massive blood loss.

The soldier, whip in hand, walk around Jesus, taunting him. Then with a mighty swing of his arm, he struck Jesus' back soundly. The blow dropped Jesus to the ground with a cry of pain. Flesh ripped as the whip was pulled back and blood flowed in rivers from the room. Brandon flinched and looked at Simeon. The angel was crying freely; his face blanched as he watched, spellbound. Brandon noticed Simeon's lips moving as though he was speaking. Brandon leaned close to hear his words.

"'Who had believed our message? To whom has the Lord's power been revealed?

"He grew up in his presence like a young tree, like a root out of dry ground.

"He had no form or majesty that would make us look at him. He had nothing in his appearance that would make us desire him.

"He was despised and rejected by people. He was a man of sorrows, familiar with suffering. He was despised like one from whom people turn their faces, and we didn't consider him to be worth anything.

"He certainly has taken upon himself our suffering and carried our sorrows, but we thought that God had wounded him, beat him, and punished him.

"He was wounded for our rebellious acts. He was crushed for our sins. He was punished so that we could have peace, and we received healing from his wounds.'"

Jennifer Wade

Simeon noticed Brandon's stare, and without being asked, he explained, "Thousands of years before this day, the prophet Isaiah spoke those words. Jesus is fulfilling prophecy."

By this time, Jesus had received most of his sentence. He lay on the ground, barely resembling a man. Blood covered His entire body and pooled beneath Him on the ground. Brandon wasn't a doctor, but even he could see that Jesus had nearly reached the point of death. Brandon left Simeon and walked to where Jesus lay in the dirt. Slowly, he knelt. Strangely, he felt that Jesus was looking straight at him. Christ had no strength to speak, but Brandon heard the words as clearly as if they had been voiced. "Brandon, these wounds are for healing. I healed your mother with these stripes. She is free of disease now and forever. Never again will she cry in pain, and never again will she need a doctor. I have made her whole."

Brandon stepped back in shock. The macabre scene was still unfolding as if nothing had taken place between himself and Jesus. No one else had heard those words. He looked back at Christ. Jesus was still staring into Brandon's eyes. One word formed on His lips as the soldiers pulled him to His feet to take Him, yet again, before Pilate. "Remember," He whispered. This time the soldier heard. His face paled as he felt the impact with Brandon.

The soldiers passed a thorn bush as they led Jesus toward the courtyard. They paused from their journey long enough to clip the vines and form them into a crown. They shoved the crown onto Christ's head, digging into the skin and causing even more bleeding. They replaced Herod's robe, draping it around the wounded body in mockery of Jesus' claim of kingship.

Now that Jesus was before Pilate for the third time, the crowd was incensed over the governor's reluctance to sentence Jesus to death. Pilate tried again to plead for Jesus' life. He whispered to his guard, and the soldier immediately left and returned with another prisoner. The man was stocky, with unkempt hair and wild eyes. The filth on his face couldn't hide the scar that ran down the side of his head, a reminder of the violence he was capable of. He had the crazed look of a maniac, and he kept moving wildly to resist the soldier's hold on his arm. This was Barabbas, a brutal killer who had been involved in many chaotic uprisings. He was slated for execution.

"My people! As you know, it is my tradition to release back to you one prisoner in honor of the Passover. I will give you a choice. Which man would you have freed? Jesus of Nazareth, a man who has done no wrong and has committed no violent act? Or Barabbas, a rioter and murderer? What say you? Whom do you chose?"

Pilate was shocked at the commotion. "Give us Barabbas!" the people cried. "Crucify Jesus!"

Pilate stepped back in confusion and despair. He did not want to kill this man. "Why should I kill Him? What has He done wrong?"

"We have a law, and by that law, He must die because He claimed to be the Son of God."

Pilate decided to talk to Jesus one last time. He had his soldiers escort Jesus into the governor's private chambers. "Where are you from?" The question was met with silence. "Aren't you going to answer me? Don't you know that I have the authority to free you or to crucify you?"

This time, Jesus spoke. "You wouldn't have any authority over me if it hadn't been given to you from above."

Pilate walked outside. The crowd was still demanding execution. "If you free this man, you're not a friend of the emperor. Anyone who claims to be a king is defying the emperor." Pilate heard their words, so he had Jesus brought outside and sat Him on the judge's seat.

"Here is your king!" Jesus was so beaten that He barely looked human. Blood covered his face and dripped onto the purple robe. His nose appeared to be broken, and His eyes were nearly swollen shut. His lips had ballooned to more than twice their normal size and were covered with blood. Every time Jesus moved His mouth, the cuts opened and fresh rivulets poured out. The sight of Him made Brandon's heart lurch.

The crowd repeated, "Free Barabbas! Crucify Jesus!"

Pilate turned toward the Jewish religious leaders. "Should I crucify your king?"

Immediately, the priests proclaimed, "The emperor is the only king we have."

Sighing, Pilate asked his manservant for a basin of water. He stepped out onto his balcony and faced the people. He looked regretfully at the prisoner. He did not want to do this, but he had no alternative. The water arrived, and Pilate dipped his hands into the cool water. "I cannot find any fault with this man. I wash my hands of this. Do what you wish."

Jesus was handed over to the soldiers with the order to crucify him. Inside the governor's mansion, Claudia's agonized "NOOOOOOO!" could be heard echoing through the massive halls.

Brandon and Simeon followed the throng of people. They watched as a heavy beam was thrown on Jesus' back. Jesus winced as the splinters from the rough wood dug into the oozing lesions on His back. He took only a few steps before the weight of the wood, combined with His weakness, caused him to stumble and fall to the ground. The soldiers surrounding Him tried to force Him back to His feet. They kicked and hit Him, endeavoring to convince Him to stand, but He was done. He had nothing left. The lack of sleep and the torturous physical maltreatments had taken everything. One soldier realized this and began to look through the crowd. His eyes fell on a muscular man in the crowd. "What is your name?" the soldier demanded.

The stranger looked around, confirming that he was the subject of the question before answering. "I am Simon. I am from the city of Cyrene. I am visiting Jerusalem for the Passover sacrifice."

"Simon of Cyrene, you look like a strong man. Carry this man's cross!"

Simon's face went ashen. "No, sir. Please, I do not wish to be a part of this."

The soldier became angry. "You will do this, or you will die." As he spoke, his hand traveled to the hilt of his sword.

Simon held up his hands in surrender. "Yes, sir." He bent and took the cross from Christ's back. "I'm sorry," he whispered.

Jesus looked at him with compassion. "This is my gift, Simon. It is meant for you as well."

Simon absorbed the words slowly, until a nudge from the guard spurred him into action. He removed the beam from the exhausted and weak form and placed it on his own shoulders. As he followed the soldiers, with Christ behind him, tears streamed down Simon's cheeks and dropped onto the ground. He had only come to Jerusalem for his annual sacrifice. He hadn't asked for this.

The stories of Jesus had reached Cyrene as well. Simon had to admit to himself that he had hoped to see Jesus while he was in the area. He hadn't known until he had seen the huge gathering of people and heard what they were saying that Jesus had been arrested. He had wanted to get out of town then, but the crowds had pressed in so much that he had been unable to turn back. Then the sight unfolding had mesmerized him. He knew that something terrible and yet strangely awesome was happening. Although he grieved as he was carrying his load, he felt peculiarly honored to be playing a part in these events.

The ragged group was led up an incline. Brandon and Simeon followed them the entire distance.

"This place is called Golgatha. It means 'place of the skull,'" Simeon said forlornly. Brandon noticed his friend's tightly clenched fists and free-flowing tears. His colorless face attested to the misery and grief he was experiencing. "We all wanted to intervene. We waited for our Father's command to stop these atrocities. The order never came."

Brandon watched in horror as Jesus was stretched out and spikes were driven through his wrists into the wood below. The cries of pain were nearly inhuman. The process was repeated on Jesus' crossed feet, and then the cross was lifted vertically and dropped into a hole to stand on its own. Jesus was struggling to breathe through the pain and seemed to pass out. Blood poured from the wounds and collected into puddles on the ground. Brandon found that his stomach was revolting at the gruesome sight. He pushed his way around Simeon and dropped to the ground, vomiting. "Why?" he asked Simeon once the sickness was past.

"Once again, I will speak the words of Isaiah," Simeon answered. "'We have all strayed like sheep. Each one of us has turned to go his own way and the Lord has laid all our sins on him.

"He was abused and punished, but he didn't open his mouth. He was led like a lamb to the slaughter. He was like a sheep that is silent when its wool is cut off. He didn't open his mouth.

"He was arrested, taken away, and judged. Who would have thought that he would be removed from the world? He was killed because of my people's rebellion. He was placed in a tomb with the wicked. He was put there with the rich when he died, although he had done nothing violent and had never spoken a lie."

Simeon paused for a moment. "Brandon, He did this for you."

CHAPTER **17**

Brandon, his stomach settled, returned to the crowd. The people were jeering and ridiculing Jesus. Christ looked around, and Brandon saw more than pain in His eyes; there was love and compassion as well. This bewildered Brandon. All grew quiet as Jesus spoke. "Father, forgive them. They do not know what they are doing."

The words confused the onlookers, and for a moment, there were silenced before chaos began again. One soldier ran to the cross with a wooden sign, holding it up for others to see. It read, "Jesus from Nazareth, the king of the Jews."

Simeon looked to Brandon. "Pilate did not want to condemn Christ to death. He was forced to. So he had this sign made, angering the Jewish leaders. They told him to change the words to 'He said that he is the king of the Jews.' Pilate refused. He said that he had written what he wanted to write and that was final. It was written in three languages so every person who was able to read would understand the words."

Brandon watched as the soldier climbed to the top of the cross and affixed the sign above Jesus' head. Then he jumped down to join his comrades at the foot of the cross as they threw dice to see who would keep Jesus' apparel.

"This was also prophesied about: 'They divided my clothes among themselves. They threw dice for my clothing.' As you can see, this came true."

The crowd continued their mockery. It was reaching the ears of the other men who were crucified with Jesus. His cross had been placed between two thieves. The thief on the left began to taunt Jesus as well. "So you're really the Messiah, are you? Well, save yourself, and us!" he sneered.

Jesus didn't respond, but the criminal on the right did. "Don't you fear God at all? Can't you see that you're condemned the same way He is? Our punishment is fair. We are getting what we deserve. But this man hasn't done anything wrong." This criminal turned to Jesus. Brandon could see regret and fear written all over his face. Quietly, the thief spoke again. "Jesus, remember me when you enter this kingdom."

Jesus faintly smiled. "I can guarantee this truth: Today, you will be with me in Paradise."

The man's face relaxed as he took in Jesus' words. "Thank you," he whispered.

About that time, several women approached the cross. The soldiers stepped in their way, preventing them from getting near. The man accompanying the women wrapped his arm around one of them. "She's his mother," he said quietly to them. The soldiers slowly moved and allowed them to step to the foot of the wooden beams. Jesus saw the women and stared at his mother. He looked over to her escort, and his lips curled upward in a vague smile. Looking back at his mother, he said, "Look, here is your son." Jesus moved his eyes to the man with his mother. Brandon recognized his as John, one of Jesus' closest friends. "Look, here is your mother."

Simeon explained to Brandon. "In this culture, a woman is dependent entirely on her husband or son. Joseph is dead, making Mary a widow. Jesus, as her oldest son, must provide for her, and He is giving His responsibility to his friend. Mary will reside with John now, and he will take care of her."

The small contingent of women with the disciple slowly gravitated away from the cross and back with the people. Brandon noticed the sky getting darker, almost as if it were getting ready to rain.

"I'm thirsty." Brandon was startled at the words coming from the cross. He watched as the soldiers soaked a sponge in some sort of liquid, placed it on a long pole, and lifted it to Jesus' lips. Christ tasted it and then turned His head.

"It is not water, Brandon. It is vinegar, and it has been mixed with gall. That was a form of painkiller used during the time," Simeon instructed.

The sky was now almost completely dark. Brandon watched the reactions from the other observers and realized they were as confused as he was. It looked to be night, although it was only midafternoon.

A loud, mournful cry came from Jesus. *"Eli, Eli, lema sabachthani?"*

Simeon whispered the translation in Brandon's ear. "It means 'My God, my God, why have You abandoned me?' Jesus has never felt separation from His Father before. He carried the sins, past present and future, of all mankind on His shoulders. Sin can't abide with God. At the same time, God is grieving and cannot watch any longer. All of Heaven is mourning with Him."

Brandon recalled feeling abandoned. Losing his mother and being left in his father's hands, he had felt like God had turned His back on him as well. He had never once thought that Jesus would have experienced the same feelings.

Brandon noticed that everyone present had gotten quiet. The mockery and ridicule from earlier had disappeared. Brandon looked up at Jesus. He wasn't moving any more, and for a moment, Brandon thought He had died. The Jesus roused enough strength to speak one more time.

"Father, into Your hands I entrust my spirit." Jesus paused briefly and then continued, "It is finished."

As soon as the words left Jesus' mouth, the ground began to shake in a violent earthquake. People began screaming and running for cover. A nearby soldier stated, "Certainly, this man was innocent!" The earth shook for several minutes, and then, just as suddenly as it had started, it stopped its wild trembling.

A temple servant came running up the hill, looking for the Jewish religious leaders. He maneuvered his way to them and tried to speak. His run had rendered him breathless, so he leaned over and put his hands on his knees, gulping air. Finally, he spoke. "Please, do not be angry. It could not be helped! The curtain, the one separating the sanctuary from the Holy of Holies, has been torn in two. The earthquake caused the damage. It cannot be repaired." The leaders looked at one another in astonishment and then turned their gazes on Jesus. Could it be?

"The veil represented the separation between God and man. Only the most holy of men could enter, and even then only after cleansing and purifying themselves. If a man had but one sin in his heart, he immediately died. Jesus has taken away that separation. Man can now freely come to God." Brandon heard Simeon's words, and they delved deeply into his brain. He certainly had a lot to think about.

The people began complaining that evening was coming soon. The Sabbath was coming, and they needed the bodies of the condemned to come off the cross. Pilate ordered that the victims' legs be broken. A soldier grabbed a club and viciously hit the legs of the first criminal. Brandon could hear the bones break and the man's cries of renewed pain. The soldier then tossed the club to another, and he did the same to the convict on the other side of Jesus. A third soldier was watching Christ. As the club-bearer came near to Him, he was stopped by another. "Wait. I think He is already dead."

The soldier with the club dropped the club and grabbed a spear. "We shall see." With that, he rammed the spear into Jesus' side. Blood mixed with water flowed from the wound. "He's gone," the Roman guard proclaimed.

Brandon looked curiously at Simeon. "Why did they break their legs?" he asked.

"Crucifixion is a cruel death. You have seen the pain and the loss of blood, but there is more to it than that. The way the arms are lifted puts strain on the lungs. To breathe, the person must push himself upright with his feet. The pain in the feet forces the person to drop down again, and the lungs renew their struggle. With their legs broken, they cannot push upward. They eventually suffocate and die. Because the holy day starts at sundown, the Jewish nation needs these men to die quickly. Their legs were broken to speed their deaths. Jesus was already dead; there was no need for this act to be carried out on Him. This fulfills yet another scripture that says, 'None of his bones will be broken.'"

Brandon watched a man dressed in the clothing of wealth approached the nearest soldier. The two of them gestured for a moment, and then the soldier nodded.

"This is Joseph, a rich man from Arimathea. He has secretly followed Jesus for quite some time. He has asked Pilate for permission to bury Jesus. Pilate agreed, and now he is here to remove the body."

Joseph climbed a rough ladder to reach Jesus' arms. He draped a length of material around His chest. The soldier nearby brought another ladder and ascended it to help. The soldier removed the spikes while Joseph held onto the material, which caught the body as it fell. The soldier then left the ladder and removed the spikes holding Jesus' feet. Joseph leaned the body forward, and the Roman received it, laying it on the ground. Brandon's attention turned as a third man joined them.

"This is Nicodemus. He is another secret follower of Christ," Simeon explained.

Together, Joseph and Nicodemus wrapped Jesus' body in strips of linen. They carried Him to a nearby garden and laid Him in a tomb that had been hewn in the rock, then they looked around for something to cover the entrance. Brandon took a moment to peer inside the sepulcher. Jesus lay on a rock slab on the side of the cool room. Customarily, these tombs held the bodies of several people, yet Jesus was alone. Apparently, this tomb was new and Jesus was the first to need it. Brandon heard scraping outside, so he turned and walked out. Joseph and Nicodemus were struggling to push a large stone to cover the doorway.

Once the rock was in place, they left. Brandon could hear them talking in low tones. Joseph said that he had to report to Pilate, telling him the location of the grave. Pilate wanted to send soldiers to guard it from thieves. Apparently, the Jewish leaders felt that some of Jesus' followers would try to steal the body and try to convince everyone that Christ had come back to life. The men conversed about the many prophesies that Jesus had told concerning this very issue.

Brandon watched the two men leave. He felt strange, as if a huge void was in his life and he didn't know how to fill it. He had watched this man teach the crowds, heal the sick, and even bring the dead back to life. He had watched the trial and the grue- some execution, and now he was sitting at the tomb of this great teacher, but what had he learned? He tried to make some sense of everything, but it seemed to flutter just beyond his reach. About the time Brandon thought he had it figured out, the answer seemed to vanish before he could fully understand it.

Simeon sat next to him, but Brandon ignored him for a moment, lost in his own thoughts. When he did ask his question, his tone was full of melancholy and depression. "So that's it. This man that taught so much and loved so greatly is dead. What's next? Jesus died alone and deserted. No one stood up in His defense. No one stopped this tragedy from hap- pening. Not Pilate, not His disciples, not even God.

You showed me that Jesus was God's Son, yet this was allowed to happen to Him? I just don't understand it."

"No, you don't. But you will."

CHAPTER 18

Brandon felt himself being lowered into a large cavernous void. The lower he went, the darker it got. He could smell burning sulphur and hear the hissing and crackling of flames. When he and Simeon finally reached the bottom, the only light came from the fires themselves, and there were many of them. The eerie glow threw dancing shadows into the recesses of what appeared to be a large cave with many tunnels.

Brandon watched as what appeared to be half man and half beast approached. The creature didn't walk so much as float. Its appearance continually changed as it moved toward them. One second, it looked almost human, the next, it appeared totally animal. It seemed to be male. The one word that Brandon would use to describe him was evil. His face was contorted into a permanent scowl of hatred, and his lips were curled in a persistent sneer of contempt.

"Where are we?" Brandon muttered under his breath.

"There are many words for this place. It has been called Hades, the Abyss, or simply a place of torment. We are in Hell."

Brandon gasped in fear, but Simeon's next words brought some relief. "You are protected. You cannot be seen, and you will not feel the heat from the flames."

"What is this creature?"

"It is a servant of the ruler of this land. Some call it a demon. It consistently changes appearance to confuse and disorient whomever it is attending. Some work calls for subtle distraction from the Truth, and so it appears gentle and beautiful. But it is a vicious monster that seeks only to destroy. There are many both here in Hell and on earth doing their master's bidding."

"Who is this master?"

"His name is Lucifer. But he is known by many names: Beelzebub, the devil, Satan. He is a most cunning adversary. He held the highest position among the angels of Heaven once. He was an extremely beautiful creation. But his pride became his obsession. He thought he was better than God. He led a rebellion, and he was sent here to await his punishment. Until then, he roams the earth, trying to keep people from God by whatever means he can. His minions obey his commands and carry out his plans of torture and deception. Together, they prey on man's weaknesses as they try to keep separation from God permanent."

Brandon looked through the shadows and saw a large throne. Although ornate, it was dark, not gold as pictures of royal thrones that Brandon had seen. It was large, and as Brandon peered closer, he could see a man slouched in it.

Brandon assumed that this was Lucifer. Even slouched as Lucifer was, Brandon could see that he was tall. He had close-cropped black hair with a thin moustache and goatee. His dark eyes held an angry yet apprehensive expression. His thick eyebrows were knitted together in a furrowed grimace. Brandon thought that the man would have been attractive were it not for his expression. His black robe dragged the ground and swirled around his feet.

"Why is he angry? He should be celebrating, as he just killed Jesus." Brandon was confused. After all, with Christ dead, people getting to God would be a nearly impossible feat. It seemed to Brandon that Lucifer had won.

"His lackeys are jubilant. They think that it is over and they have achieved victory. But Lucifer knows God very well. He is sure that God has a plan and things aren't exactly finished yet."

As soon as Simeon said this, Brandon heard a loud bang coming from the closest tunnels. Lucifer leapt to his feet at the sound. He stared nervously down the corridor as a holy light filled the unhallowed dwelling. The bang came again, only this time it was much louder. Simeon, Brandon, and Lucifer watched in unison as an enormous gate was flung through the room as though it weighed nothing more than a feather. Brandon's jaw dropped in amazement as Simeon merely smiled. Lucifer's reaction though, was much different.

The fallen angel appeared agitated. He nervously watched the tunnel for any more movement. Beads of sweat appeared on his forehead, and he wiped them away in annoyance. Brandon found himself chuckling as Lucifer dried his hands on his robe. Whatever the cause of this disturbance, it was severely affecting Lucifer.

The light grew brighter, and soon it had enveloped the entire room. Brandon heard eerie screams coming from the surrounding tunnels. He noticed a couple of Lucifer's minions slinking further down the recesses, hiding in fear. Brandon was shielding his eyes, trying to see where the light was coming from, but then it suddenly vanished. He blinked his eyes as they adjusted and was deeply surprised to see Jesus Himself standing in the room. Brandon looked around for Lucifer. He was cowering at Christ's feet, groveling for mercy.

"Wh-what are you d-doing here?" he stammered. "'This is my domain!"

"And so it shall stay."

Brandon had not heard this majestic quality in Jesus' voice before. It was the same intonation he had heard several times before, yet now there was power and authority behind the tone.

"I am merely here for a simple task." Jesus continued. "I want the keys!"

"What keys?" Lucifer stalled.

"You know which keys I speak of. But to clarify, I want the keys to death and the grave."

"They are mine!" Lucifer argued.

"Not anymore," Jesus stated simply. "I have bought them with my own blood. You will relinquish them."

Angry but defeated, Lucifer reached inside his robe and withdrew an ancient ring of keys. "Take them and be gone!"

Jesus grabbed the keys, and in an instant, He was gone. Lucifer, still on his knees, wailed into the darkness. The anguished sounds reverberated through every inch of Hell, causing demons to scurry around in alarm. They knew their master would be working hard to get his retribution. They had to be prepared for his attack.

"That was intense!" Brandon exclaimed as the darkness of Hell transformed into the early rays of dawn.

"It is not over yet."

Brandon noticed that they were back in the garden sepulcher that housed the body of Jesus. Several Roman soldiers were guarding the grave. The sight of the warriors and of the stone covering the entrance of the tomb reminded Brandon of the horrendous images he had witnessed.

"It really happened, didn't it?" he asked softly. "Jesus is really dead."

"Yes. Jesus was really killed. He suffered greatly, and then He gave the greatest gift mankind would ever know. There was a verse written by the Apostle John that has always been one of my favorites. It says, 'Greater love has no man than this, that he lay down his life for a friend.' There is so much truth to those simple words, yet I think Christ's gift was even greater. He gave His life willingly for those He loved, yes, but He also died for those who hated and rejected Him."

"I guess it would be hard to die in someone else's place. It would be even harder if that person had done me wrong," Brandon replied.

"You just saw Jesus take the keys of death and the grave from Lucifer. Now you can see what those keys can do."

At that instant, Brandon felt a ripple under his feet. The entire area started trembling. The soldiers looked toward the stone just as a tremendous light shot out from its edges. The large rock started shaking and then was shoved to the side by an unseen hand. The soldiers' reactions were fierce. Every one of them fell down in a fright-induced slumber. Brandon watched in awe as dust settled around the tomb.

It was then that he heard the sound of approaching footsteps on the leaf-covered path.

Three women were nearing the grave. Brandon recognized the mother of Jesus. He had seen the other two before, in the crowds surrounding Christ. They were carrying jars, and Brandon could smell the spicy aroma emanating from them.

"They have come to prepare the body. They could not do this earlier because of the holy day of rest. They come now, but they will not see what they are expecting." Simeon pointed to the stone. It sat lopsided at the opening in the rock wall. The women arrived and were shocked to see the stone moved. They began to murmur amongst themselves as to why this was. One woman suggested that the soldiers knew they were coming and had moved this obstacle in advance. They ducked into the opening, and then Brandon heard their cries of alarm. Before the women could exit the tomb, a man dressed in white settled himself on the stone and waited. When the women stepped out of the tomb, the man spoke to them.

"Why are you looking among the dead for the Living One? He is not here. He has been brought back to life! Remember what He told you while He was still in Galilee."

Brandon watched as each woman sank to the ground at the man's words. He could see that they were recalling Jesus' words and the realization was heavy upon them.

The man continued, "He said, 'The Son of Man must be handed over to sinful people, be crucified, and come back to life on the third day.'"

The women ran from the tomb. Brandon could hear their excited chatter until they had run too far for their words to reach him. The words were clear; the women were going to tell the disciples what they had just heard. When the garden was silent again, Brandon took a moment to gape into the roughly carved tomb for himself.

The room was dark and cold. The flat boulder that Jesus' body had lain on was empty, except for the linen strips Joseph and Nicodemus had carefully wrapped Jesus in. They were tossed carelessly to the side. The cloth that had covered Christ's face was folded and placed where His head had been.

"Where is He?" Brandon asked.

"You heard the angel speak. He isn't here. You saw Him take the keys of death and the grave from Lucifer. Jesus has power over death. He has risen from the dead."

Brandon heard approaching footsteps again, only this time, they sounded heavier and they were running. A man, breathing heavily, burst through the tomb's entrance. Brandon knew that this was Peter. Peter paused as he surveyed the small room in the sepulcher. He walked to the strips of linen and slowly reached to pick them up. He brought them to his face as he began to sob. Another disciple, John, slowly entered the tomb behind Peter. He sat down on the narrow stone bed and picked up the head covering. He was crying too, but not as openly as Peter. Together, they left.

Brandon and Simeon slipped out of the tomb and followed Peter and John. They led them to a house. Peter knocked, and the door was opened.

"Emotions are high right now. Anyone who followed Jesus is hiding for fear of arrest. The disciples are here, behind locked doors, trying to be safe." Brandon nodded his understanding as they entered the room.

Peter, John, and Mary were in the middle of the cramped room. They were explaining what they had seen at the tomb. Several people wept as they tried to figure out who would have stolen Christ's body. The three women who had arrived there first were adamant that no theft had occurred. Mary kept insisting that Jesus had come back to life. No one was really listening to her. They thought that it was wishful thinking, brought on by grief. The ensuing argument became loud and abrasive.

Brandon felt a wind stirring in the room. He looked to the doors and windows, but they were all closed tight. One by one, the others in the room could feel the breeze too. They stopped their bickering as they looked at one another in confusion. Then Brandon noticed a light spreading through the room. He recognized it; he had seen it before. The light grew bright before it vanished. In its place stood

Jesus Himself. Everyone dropped to their knees both astonishment and reverence.

"Peace be with you." Brandon knew this voice. It was the compassionate yet authoritative tone that he had heard command Lucifer in Hell. He watched as Jesus showed His friends the wounds in His hands and feet as proof that it was really Him. Then He commanded them to tell others about Him, saying, "As the Father has sent me, so I am sending you."

The noise in the room faded away. Brandon was still there, but he could not hear anything. Simeon spoke to him, and Brandon heard not only with his ears but also with his heart. "This is a command for everyone. How will people hear if they are not told? Lydia did this for you. She lived and talked the truth. Now that you have seen, it will be your turn. I must leave now. My time with you is finished." With those words, Simeon disappeared and Brandon was left alone.

CHAPTER 19

Brandon plunged downward through the earth. He knew he was headed toward Hell again, and the thought scared him. Simeon was gone, and with him went Brandon's protection. As Brandon got closer, the familiar smell of sulphur assaulted his nose and screams of torment assailed his ears. He remembered the smell, but the sounds were new. They served to frighten him even more as they got louder the farther downward he went.

He landed with a harsh thud, and for a moment, he lay there. The heat was oppressive, and flames surrounded him on all sides. Once again, shadows moved in merriment, hiding the creatures that walked this territory. He called out, trying to find solace, but the only answer he heard was the crackling of fire and the sadistic chuckles from the demonic inhabitants.

Brandon stood on his feet. He turned around repeatedly, attempting to find the source of the evil laughs, but he could see nothing, and his frail endeavors only served to make the giggles louder. It was as if the beasts knew he was scared and they were thriving on it. The screams of pain around him were causing extreme anxiety for him as he feared what would become of him.

Nearing panic, Brandon cried out, "Jesus!" There was no answer. He tried again, "Jesus!" This time, the response was instantaneous, only it wasn't from Christ. An unseen hand shoved him backward, and he landed soundly in the middle of a nearby blaze. The fire scorched Brandon's skin, and he pulled back, astonished to see that no physical evidence of an injury could be seen. There was no blister, no red area, nothing to show the trauma. He quickly stood and moved away from the orange and blue flames. A loud voice angrily boomed, "That name has no power here!"

"Who are you, and where are you hiding?" Brandon tried to mask the terror in his voice, but it was a failed attempt.

"Who I am doesn't matter, but I know who you are, Brandon Moore!"

Brandon took an unconscious step backward at the sound of his name.

"Ah, yes. I can see that you are uncomfortable with my knowledge. Allow me to go further. You are the son of Robert Moore, a man most definitely in my control. I worked hard to keep the truth from him, as I have you. I spent years perfecting my plan. Abuse is always a great way to continue a circle of hate and sin. Now you are here, and you are mine!"

"No. My grandmother prays for me! I cannot be here!"

"Your grandmother's prayers are useless now. She may have hurled some obstacles in my way, but in the end, I prevailed."

Brandon was surprised to hear this. He knew that he had rebelled against God, but he had thought that his grandmother's prayers would have made some difference in the situation he was in now. "Oh God, please help me now," he fervently prayed. For the first time in his adult life, he meant every word.

Lydia woke with a start. How could she have fallen asleep? She silently berated herself for her weakness. She had been having a nightmare. She had felt the heat of flames, and she had heard Brandon's voice coming from within them. She knew he was in trouble.

"Oh God, what do I do?" Lydia was nearing hysteria as she jumped out of bed.

"Pray." She heard the voice audibly. Lydia grabbed her Bible and knelt beside the bed as she began pouring her heart out to her Father. The Lord whispered again, and she turned her Bible to the Psalms. A prayer from the pages rose to her heart as she read them out loud.

"Turn your ear toward me, O LORD. Answer me, because I am oppressed and needy.

"Protect me, because I am faithful to you. Save your servant who trusts you. You are my God.

"Have pity on me, O Lord, because I call out to you all day long.

"Give me joy, O Lord, because I lift my soul to you.

"You, O Lord, are good and forgiving, full of mercy toward everyone who calls out to you.

"Open your ears to my prayer, O LORD. Pay attention when I plead for mercy.

"When I am in trouble, I call out to you because you answer me.

"No god is like you, O Lord. No one can do what you do.

"All the nations that you have made will bow in your presence, O Lord. They will honor you.

"Indeed, you are great, a worker of miracles. You alone are God.

"Teach me your way, O LORD, so that I may live in your truth. Focus my heart on fearing you.

"I will give thanks to you with all my heart, O Lord my God. I will honor you forever because your mercy toward me is great. You have rescued me from the depths of hell.

"O God, arrogant people attack me, and a mob of ruthless people seeks my life. They think nothing of you.

"But you, O Lord, are a compassionate and merciful God. You are patient, always faithful and ready to forgive.

"Turn toward me, and have pity on me. Give me your strength because I am your servant. Save me because I am the son of your female servant.

"Grant me some proof of your goodness so that those who hate me may see it and be put to shame. You, O LORD, have helped me and comforted me.'" Lydia paused. "Oh God, protect Brandon. He is in need of You now, more than ever before. I trust You, my God. I will praise Your name."

Lydia steadfastly remained in prayer. She determined to continue her petitions until God released her and she knew Brandon was safe.

Brandon watched as the creatures of Hell drew closer. They were dragging heavy links of chains. The metal clanked as it slid over the hard ground. There were four demonic beings surrounding him, taunting him with their instruments of bondage.

"Oh God! Where are you?"

"He is not here. He has deserted you." As they talked, they wrapped the bulky chains around Brandon. The more they wrapped, the harder it was for Brandon to stand under the weight. The chains looped over his shoulders and around his chest. These were held in place with large, ancient padlocks. Smaller chains wrapped around his wrists and ankles, and then they too were locked in place. Brandon was completely immobilized. The creatures then picked Brandon up, held him over their heads, and carried him to a nearby pocket in the surrounding wall. Here, they unceremoniously dumped him in the corner and locked him inside the recess.

Brandon lay on the burning ground, weeping. He had never felt so alone in his life. He was terrified that the demons would return. His thoughts swirled around everything he had seen and heard as Simeon had guided him through his past and given him the miracle of seeing Jesus face to face. Rachel and Lydia had taught him from a young age about the Bible. He had heard the stories, but he had actually been given the gift of being there to watch as things unfolded. He now had nothing but regrets as he tried desperately to think of a way out of Hell.

"God? Are You there? Can You see me? Can You help me?" Brandon choked the words out as he drifted off into a tortured slumber.

Lydia breathed a sigh of relief. She still had no idea what was happening with Brandon, but she knew that God was in control and that Brandon would be fine.

"It is nearly over, Lydia," the gentle voice whispered in her ear.

"Thank you, Lord," she cried. Then she quoted her favorite psalm from the Bible. "The LORD is my shepherd. I am never in need.

"He makes me lie down in green pastures. He leads me beside peaceful waters.

"He renews my soul. He guides me along the paths of righteousness for the sake of his name.

"Even though I walk through the dark valley of death, because you are with me, I fear no harm. Your rod and your staff give me courage.

"You prepare a banquet for me while my enemies watch. You anoint my head with oil. My cup overflows.

"Certainly, goodness and mercy will stay close to me all the days of my life, and I will remain in the LORD'S house for days without end." She finished the psalm by saying, "Amen, Lord. Amen."

CHAPTER **20**

Brandon jolted awake. He was in his room, lying on his bed. The makeshift prison and flames were gone. Had it all been a dream? He was still dressed in the jeans and t-shirt that he had fallen asleep in. In confusion, he looked out the window. It was still dark. The wind had stopped blowing, so the storm must have passed. He sat up.

He tried to reach for his clock to check the time, but his arms wouldn't move. He attempted to stand, but he couldn't move his legs either. The only movement his body would allow was the raising and lowering of his upper body and the turning of his head.

"What is going on?" Brandon asked, both stupefied and slightly scared.

"The physical chains are gone, Brandon, but you are still spiritually bound."

Brandon was startled to hear someone with him in his bedroom. He moved his head in the direction of the voice and gasped. He had expected to find Simeon, but instead, he was face to face with God.

The figure sat in the lone chair in Brandon's room. The chair was in the corner, next to the closet. Moonlight drifted in the windows and cast its light over the form sitting there. God leaned forward, his elbows on his knees and his hands clasped together.

"You've had quite a journey tonight, son." God stated. "It is nearing an end, but at the same time, it is approaching a new beginning. The question is, will you take the step?"

"How can I take any steps when I can't even move?"

God smiled. He waved His hand, and Brandon felt a weight fall from his body. Tentatively, Brandon lifted one hand as if to test his freedom. From habit, he popped his knuckles and stretched as he rose from the bed.

"Do you have any questions for me, Brandon?"

Brandon hesitated for a moment. He had experienced an extraordinary night, but he still hurt from the things in his past. "Why did you take her?"

"There are many times when I choose to heal in an earthly life. There are also times when I take my child home for an eternal healing. Either way, the promised healing arrives. I have counted every hair on the head of every person in the world, past, present, and future. I also know the number of days given to everyone to live. Rachel's days were completed. She was ready for her eternal home. She is happy there, she is with me, and she has no pain. Would you really want her here suffering? I could have healed her and left her here, but there is still the suffering of life—hunger, poverty, pain—it's everywhere you look. But her eyes behold nothing like that. What life would you prefer her to lead?"

"You make a valid point. She wanted Heaven. I heard her talk about it many times. But why did I have to go with my dad?"

"I hoped that you would help your dad heal. That was my plan. But my enemy had a strong hold on Robert, and he was unwilling to let go. Robert made his own choices. Free will is a gift I gave to man. It hurt deeply when he chose rebellion."

God rose and moved to where Brandon was standing. "I walked with Adam in the garden. I conversed with him daily. He and Eve were tricked by the master of deception. I heard the echo of the fruit crunching in their mouths. I thought it was the sound of my own heart breaking. Never again could I dwell with my creation. We were alienated from each other, so I had to take drastic measures to bring us together again."

"So You sent Jesus."

"Yes. I sent my only Son. You see, only a spotless sacrifice could take away sins. For centuries past, my people had slaughtered animals to wash them clean of their sins, but as these sacrifices were regularly made, I longed for a simpler, yet permanent, way to bring me and my beloved children together again. Jesus made the way."

"His death was horrific." Brandon shuddered as he remembered the violence and the blood.

"Yes, it was. I couldn't watch. My Son was suffering, and the weight of every sin known to man separated us for the first time. It was devastating for me. My angels begged Me to allow them to intervene. But I could not grant their desires. It was the only way." God paused for a moment. "Let me show you what I mean."

Brandon felt a violent shaking under his feet. He remembered the earthquake at the cross. He fell to his knees and protectively covered his head. When the quaking stopped, he lifted his face. His bedroom was gone. He was on a sandy cliff. God was nowhere to be seen.

Brandon scrambled to his feet and looked frantically to see where he was. He carefully crept to the edge of the cliff and looked down. He was several hundred feet high. He would never be able to go down without severe injury or death. He was lost.

"I am here, Brandon." He heard God's voice, even though he couldn't see Him. "Look past the cliff."

Brandon stood still and stared past the steep edge. He shielded his eyes, and in the far distance, he could barely make out the shape of another precipice.

"This chasm represents the separation that sin has caused. Just like the physical chains that bound you in hell and the spiritual chains you felt a moment ago, it keeps you from approaching me."

Brandon could barely see the other cliff, much less God standing on it, yet the words sounded as if God were right next to him.

"As things look now, Brandon, how would you get to me?"

Brandon answered honestly. "I couldn't. Not by myself, anyway."

"You're right. In your own power, you can't reach me. Many people have tried. But there is only one bridge that can span the distance. I provided it, and it stands next to you."

Brandon glanced around. He didn't remember seeing a bridge when he stood at the brink of the rocky cliff. He looked again and confirmed his suspicions. There was no bridge. What was God talking about? Then he saw it.

To the side, almost hidden with shrubbery and overgrown vines, stood a familiar sight. Tears welled in Brandon's eyes, and he swallowed the lump in his throat. He moved through the underbrush until he reached it.

Here stood a bloody cross.

Brandon's tears slipped free from his eyes. He reached out his hand and rubbed the splintery beams. He had seen Jesus heal. He had heard the compassionate voice as Jesus had spoken of love. He had watched as Christ had made the broken whole and restored life.

He recalled the feeling of betrayal as he had watched Judas give Jesus over to the authorities. He could still hear the crowd demanding Jesus' death. He remembered Pilate's pleas for pardon. The sound of the whips ripping flesh hit Brandon's heart as he fell to his knees.

The final moments of Jesus' life replayed over and over in Brandon's head. He remembered how Jesus had taken time, even while on the cross, to make sure that His mother was cared for after His death. Then in the end, He had willingly died, when He could have so easily spared Himself the agony and pain of death.

Brandon's hands brushed something soft. He leaned down and saw a single red rose growing right in front of the rough wood. Gently, he leaned over and sniffed the fragrant scent. He heard God's voice. "A rose is a delicate flower. It can only be cultivated by experienced hands. It is a flower often used for love and romance. It is fitting that a rose is here, for it shows my love for you. Did you know, however, that although the rose has a fragrant bloom, the most powerful scent can only be smelled when the petals are crushed? That is also representative of my gift of love. The true aroma can only be experienced with sacrifice. I gave my Son to you. I leave my offering in your hands."

Brandon thought for a moment. He recalled the grief he had felt in losing his mother. He thought about the pain he had experienced at his father's hand.

For a moment, anger and bitterness swelled inside his chest. Then he thought about Lydia. She had done whatever it had taken to get him back to safety. She had covered him in prayer and had enlisted others to pray with her on his behalf. His mind turned to Officer Higgins and Mr. Evans. Godly people had been with him through every aspect of his life. That couldn't have been an accident.

Brandon was tired. He was exhausted with the effort of staying angry and arguing with God. It was time to give up. He whispered the words. "I accept Your offering. If You will have me, then I am Yours."

Instantly, the cross began to grow. Brandon sat on his behind in the dust as the cross continued to grow high into the sky. He could no longer see the top of it, and he could no longer look around it. It was enormous. Then, with an ear-splitting crack, the base of the beam broke and the cross came crashing down.

Brandon threw his arm over his face until the dust settled. When everything was clear, he rose to his feet. He gazed upon the sight in total awe. The cross had fallen perfectly and bridged the gap between the two cliffs. The deep chasm now had a path for Brandon to navigate.

"You can come to me now." God's gentle voice gave Brandon the push he needed to move to the new bridge. Brandon hesitated before taking the first step.

"I understand. This is new and you are scared. It only takes one step. The next one will be easier. I am waiting here for you, and I am patient. Do not fear me, for I love you."

Brandon took a tentative step. His eyes blurred, and he impatiently wiped away the tears. He was leaving his old life for a new one. The thought brought a bundle of nerves, but he was sure of one thing—he was loved. God had proven it, just as Brandon had asked Him to. Brandon knew this life would not be perfect or free from trouble, but he would have God by his side, and that would make the effort worth it.

Brandon took a deep breath and ventured ahead for a second step, then a third. God was barely in view, but Brandon could see him bouncing up and down in anticipation. The sight made Brandon momentarily freeze as the impact hit. God was excited about this. Brandon was just a simple man. He could not boast of fame or major accomplishments, but yet God was anticipating his arrival. The thought humbled Brandon even more as he realized his worth in God's eyes.

He started walking again, but he could not take his eyes off of his Father. The closer Brandon got, the more anxious God became. Brandon began giggling like a little child waiting for Christmas. He couldn't stop, and soon, laughter consumed him. He could hear God laughing with him.

Then, all at once, God stopped his merriment. He spoke one word, "Brandon," then He ran toward Brandon. God reached Brandon and held him tightly against His chest. "I couldn't wait any more. This day has been too long in coming."

Brandon wept for joy as he clung to God. He was astonished to feel God's tears falling and mixing with his own. Brandon felt himself falling, and his knees hit the wooden beam beneath him. God lowered Himself too, refusing to release his new child.

Time held no meaning as the two stayed together. Brandon found himself staring at the cross under his knees. Right there, between him and God, was a blood stain. He gasped and met God's eyes. God simply nodded as the realization dawned on Brandon. Here he was, with God, the blood that sealed their covenant connecting them.

Fresh tears assailed Brandon's eyes as he whispered, "Thank you."

CHAPTER 21

Brandon sat at the kitchen table. His tears had dried, and his time with God had ended all too soon. He watched out the window as the sun shone its first rays across the horizon. The storm had been turbulent through the night, but the morning was coming fresh and clean. Brandon thought it symbolic for the way he felt at this moment too.

He wanted to wake Lydia, to tell her what had happened to him, but he felt reluctant to do so. His emotions were still raw, and anything brought new tears to his eyes. He still needed time to reflect on the previous night, as well as on the change that had occurred in him. He would find something to fix for breakfast, and then he would wake Lydia.

Brandon rummaged through his cabinets to see what he had available. He had a couple of frying pans, but that was it. His refrigerator held the necessary ingredients for a world-class omelet, but he didn't know how to make one. He grabbed his car keys, scribbled a note for Lydia in case she woke, and left the apartment.

He started his car, pulled out of the parking lot, and headed to the twenty-four–hour Walmart. He should be able to find some cooking supplies there. He would make his purchases and surprise Lydia with a decent breakfast.

Brandon grabbed a buggy and pushed it toward the kitchen appliances. There, wedged in between microwaves and toasters, he found one omelet maker. That would be perfect. He placed it in the cart, threw in a spatula and a mixer, and was ready to pay for his items. He rounded the corner and stopped short. "Mr. Evans!" Brandon sputtered in surprise. "What are you doing here this early?"

"I couldn't sleep. Something kept urging me to come here, so I got dressed and left the house. I don't even want to buy anything." Mr. Evans felt a stirring in his spirit. "You look different, Brandon. Is everything all right? I remember that your grandmother was coming for a visit."

Brandon knew this had to be the hand of God. "Actually, she is at my apartment, sleeping. I had an interesting night, and I wanted to surprise her with breakfast this morning. I felt I needed to kind of make up for the argument we had last night."

"Do you want to talk about it?" Mr. Evans had always been a kind man, ready to help whenever he was needed.

"You know, I really would, but I can't right now. I'll just say that both you and Gram were right. I've come home. That's what I wanted to tell Gram this morning. Why don't you come for breakfast, too? That way I only have to tell my story once. And maybe you could help me learn to use this thing?" Brandon pointed to the omelet maker and sheepishly shrugged.

Mr. Evans laughed. "If it involves food, I'll be there."

Brandon paused for a moment. "I do have a favor to ask. I feel like I need to head back to Virginia for a while. Do you think that I could have a leave of absence?"

"I think that can be arranged. Take all the time you need."

Brandon breathed a sigh of relief. God was preparing a way for him to take care of some things. "Thanks. I really appreciate it."

Brandon took care of his purchases, and then Mr. Evans followed him to the apartment.

About an hour later, Lydia woke to the sounds of men laughing in the kitchen. She recognized Brandon's hearty laugh and nearly cried. When was the last time she had heard him laugh with such abandon? She was confused about the other voice, though. Brandon hadn't told her he was expecting company this morning.

She rose and quickly dressed. Something was going on, and she intended to find out what it was.

Lydia walked down the hallway and stepped into the kitchen. She was shocked to see the mess it was in. Dirty bowls cluttered the counters, the sink was filled with utensils, and eggshells and cheese littered the floor.

"What is going on?" she stammered.

Brandon and Mr. Evans looked at her, then at each other, and then collapsed into another fit of laughter.

Brandon finally composed himself enough to say, "We were trying to fix omelets. Gram, this is my boss, Mr. Evans. Tom Evans, this is my gram, Lydia Stevens."

Mr. Evans dried his hands on his pants and then extended one to shake Lydia's. "It's good to finally meet you in person, Lydia."

"You too, Tom. Now, will someone please tell me what is going on?"

Brandon looked slightly embarrassed as he simply said, "We were making breakfast. We wanted to surprise you." Mr. Evans coughed, attempting to hide yet another chuckle.

"I guess I'd better finish, or we'll be calling the fire department. Go set down at the table, and I'll be finished in just a few minutes." Lydia shuffled then to the chairs and got to work. She started a pot of coffee, and soon the rich aroma filled the small kitchen. In no time, the small room was clean and plates were filled with hearty ham-and-cheese omelets. Mr.

Evans bowed his head to thank God for the food, and the three of them ate with fervor.

As the eggs disappeared, Brandon found himself growing nervous. He had always written his feelings down instead of speaking them. The story he had to tell was unbelievable at best, but he knew it must be told.

Finally, he cleared his throat and began. "I have a story to tell, and it will be hard for you to conceive of. First, let me say that I am sorry for all the grief that you two experienced over me. I know now that there is a God and He loves me very much." He had thought he had his emotions under control, but he felt them now just under the surface, ready to break as he spoke.

Lydia and Mr. Evans sat back in their chairs. They glanced at each other, understanding that whatever had happened to Brandon had been extraordinary. They waited as Brandon struggled with his tears and words before continuing.

"I thought that my world was over when my mom died. The pain from that shadowed everything, even the abuse from my dad. After living with my father for those two years, my heart became very hard. As you both know, I felt that if God existed, then my family should be intact and happy. My mom would be alive and my dad wouldn't be a violent drunk. But I was wrong. I have learned during the night that God was with me every step of the way as I grew, even when I refused to acknowledge Him."

Lydia sat up straight in her chair. "Brandon, I was awake most of the night, praying for you. I never heard you move. What happened during the night that has caused this reversal? Don't misunderstand what I am saying—I am thrilled at this revelation; I am just very confused."

"I guess I'd better start from the beginning. Do you remember the start of the thunderstorm last night?" Brandon told the whole story from the eerie sensation at the brewing storm, to Simeon's appearance, to his final dialogue with God at the cliffs. Lydia and Mr. Evans sat, enthralled, from Brandon's first word to his last. Coffee went ignored and grew cold as their attention focused, unwavering on Brandon's narration.

"I saw a lot during the night, and no, it wasn't a vivid dream. These things were real, and my life has been changed," Brandon said as he concluded his story.

For a moment, no one spoke, then Lydia broke the silence. "I believe you."

Brandon glanced up, surprised.

Lydia continued, "I knew there was something important going to happen during the night. First, the whole reason I came here was that God told me that He was going to do a miracle in you. I had an experience myself on the way here. I didn't tell you about it earlier, because I knew you would think that I was making it up." Lydia recounted her time with the taxi driver. "He said that you would need my prayers, so after I went to my room last night, I started fulfilling my promise. I lay down for a little while, when I felt some peace, but then I woke up, knowing that you were in trouble. I prayed again, until I knew that you were okay. I believe you, Brandon."

"I do, too," Mr. Evans added. "I couldn't sleep either. I knew something was wrong, but I just didn't know what it was. I was praying, too, except my prayers were general. I hadn't been given a name. Then God told me to get up and go to Walmart. He wanted us to meet."

Brandon smiled at the people who shared the table with him. He loved them both. Gram had been there for him his entire life, if only in prayer, and Mr. Evans had been a wonderful boss and great friend. He jolted as he recalled the story Lydia had recounted.

"What did you say the name of the taxi driver was?"

"It was really different. Simeon. That's it."

Brandon's tears started anew. "That's him! That's the angel God sent to guide me during the night!"

The three of them sat around the table praising God for several minutes before Brandon spoke again. "Gram, I'm coming back with you. There are some things I need to do. Mr. Evans has graciously given me a leave of absence."

Lydia was surprised, but she said nothing. Like Mary when presented with gifts for the newborn king, she held these things in her heart.

EPILOGUE

Simeon once again was treading the golden pathways leading to the Throne Room. His mission completed, he smiled as he thought of the outcome. They had experienced success, and Heaven was rejoicing.

He pulled open the massive doors and entered the room. All twenty-four leaders turned their heads in unison, wanting to hear his story. He bowed before his King. "Father, our task is complete, and we experienced victory. There is much celebration in the streets at the news. A new child has come home."

God smiled. He remembered the time He had spent with Brandon at His Son's cross. Yes, the endeavor had been hard to endure, but the outcome was perfect. He reached beside Himself and retrieved an enormous golden book. Simeon knew it to be the Lamb's Book of Life. God opened the heavy covering and turned the pages until He found the right one. He angled it so Simeon could see what was written. There, in the middle of the page, written in blood, was the name Brandon Moore. Simeon had known it would be there, but seeing it written made him dance with joy.

Simeon's excitement was contagious, and soon, everyone was dancing in praise to their King. A new soul added to the book always caused merriment and praise to the inhabitants of Heaven.

God sobered first. He looked straight at Simeon. "There is still much to be done. I have paved the way for Brandon to accompany Lydia when she returns home. It will not be for a brief visit. Brandon is about to experience more change than he realizes. He will not return to Florida. I have someone else coming to help Mr. Evans. Brandon will fulfill his mission in the mountains of Virginia, where he is from."

"What do I need to do, Father?" The question was immediate. Simeon knew he had more work to do.

"Prepare the way. Put the thought in a certain nurse. She will hear and obey."

"Yes, Father." Simeon bowed low and then turned to exit the room. His new mission would not be an easy one. The son had returned home, but the father had been held by Satan's influence for a very long time. Those chains would be difficult to break. Would Heaven be rejoicing again? He looked up and caught the eye of a young woman. Her dark hair draped around her shoulders as she participated in the celebrations of her son's homecoming. Rachel winked at Simeon as he walked past. Yes, Simeon would do everything he could to help Robert find his way home.

FROM THE AUTHOR

I see a gaping hole within your soul.
Let me fill it up for you and make you whole.
I know how dry the desert is you're in.
Let me give you living water from within.
I know how long you struggle in your life.
Won't you let me put my peace in you tonight?
I paid the price for you so long ago.
Why won't you let me in your heart and soul?
I'm right here when you feel the time is near.
Just open up your heart and know I'm here.
I'll walk the road with you through thick and thin,
So don't be afraid, my child, just let me in.
I am all you need, and I can set you free.
Please don't make me wait for you.

I wrote these words several years ago. I had never before written poetry, but I really felt that God had given me this for a purpose. Finally, a friend, Jon Gray, helped me make some changes and polish things the way they should be. Jon is a songwriter for his band, Last Days, and they took what God had given me and turned it into song. You can find more information on their ministry by visiting their web site, www.lastdaysgospel.org.

I want to thank everyone who has supported and prayed for me during the process of completing this book. You are too numerous to count, but thanks to my family, my friends, my pastor, and my church family. You all mean the world to me. And I especially want to thank God for giving me a vision, and the ability to see it fulfilled.

CPSIA information can be obtained at www.ICGtesting.com
Printed in the USA
238306LV00001B/2/P